The Inspirational Thinking of the Aesthetics of Artistic Principle
- 2018 Lee Yi-han Simulated Images

新道美學 靈動思惟

2018李憶含觀象擬真

李憶含　著

李憶含藝術工作室　出版

雄獅美術　編製

目錄

李憶含貫串古今兼顧中西的多元文化創作觀

—— 王哲雄

前臺灣師範大學美術系主任暨研究所所長
法國巴黎第四大學西洋藝術史與考古學博士

中國水墨畫的未來發展，何去何從？這已經不是新鮮的問題。然而，時值「千禧年」帶來的心理焦躁與徨惑，這個得不到滿意答案的老問題，在即將邁入公元兩千年的當今，又再度地被提起，並且以前所未有的關切和期盼，努力從事腦力的激盪，或許可以理出一些比較清晰的概念，作為另一個「千年」開始的時候繼續推研的目標。

李憶含就是活在當下焦灼而不明確的時代，所以他要思考的事物比別人更多更複雜。一向好學上進又肯用腦思索的他，早就不把中國水墨畫侷限在一個單向思維模式去詮釋；只要援引他所條列的創作理念若干句，就不難體驗李憶含唯恐「思有失縝密」的焦慮。茲略引數條如下：

（一）古今精神轉化，中西思想匯通。
（二）結合多元文化，創造民族特色。
（三）反映生活現實，傳達時代見證。
（四）根源生命體驗，呈現內在情思。
（五）理解藝術脈絡，反映歷史真相。
（六）感應現代思想，探索心靈本質。

單就以上這六條，已經大大的超過了傳統水墨畫該含容的特質。「後現代」的這一代，世紀末的徵候尤其明顯，李憶含的創作理念和他的作品就是最好的證明。〈智性思維〉是李憶含為了探討社會規範中，群體和自我互相依存的關係，藉此影射：人在自我意識的表態中要理性。該作品在形式上的確使用相當理性的圓弧、方形、垂直和水平之幾何形體與線性結構等元素，組成嚴密相扣的「結構主義」的冷漠畫面，這正是「社會體制」的規範常態。李憶含中體西用、多元文化的思辨，已經讓他跨開東方水墨與西方繪畫之間的藩籬。

〈思想神化〉一作，是李憶含有感於世紀末亂象橫生，祈求累積千年智慧思想的中國文化道統，盼思想神化以示悟明救世之道。象徵古聖賢思想道統的雕柱，周圍呈龍蛇狀攀爬浮昇的幻象，以及類似佛門法輪顯像的情境，是以西方超現實主義的手法來表現的，結構鬆緊有度，仰角透視有望之彌高的神化誘因，是一幅經營成功的作品。

〈屹立長存〉基本上是將天地萬物的秩序納入抽象的邏輯思考，萬物的表象與精神象徵，原本就有它特定依存運轉的軌道，如日月之運行。李憶含以抽象表現主義的形式，使用水墨暈染拓畫，間採立體主義的結構與象徵主義的符號，並列呈現，渾然一氣：「古今本相續，中外何需分」。

最後，例舉〈文明省思〉一幅畫作，作為本文的結束。該畫是李憶含處身科技主導時期，深深感覺到人類生活體式與價值觀有急遽的改變，此種改變往往與自然觀相違抗衡，致使「文明」的意義迷失。科技如果沒有文明的支撐，人類將會掉入另一次未開發的野蠻時期。李憶含以超現實的圖式、象徵主義的語彙，描繪人類的一隻魔掌正伸入奧秘的宇宙，是福是禍端賴省思再三，警世之言溢於畫表。

李憶含的畫作，極富思想性與文學性，他能貫串古今中外的思想和技法，也表現出相當程度的成熟度，如果能在素材運用上開拓更多元的嘗試，假以時日，必有大成。

Lee Yi-han's creative multiculturalism that transcends both the ancient and contemporary times as well as breakthroughs oriental and occidental boundary

Wang Jhe-syong

Doctor of Western Arts History and Archaeology, Université Paris-Sorbonne (Paris IV)
Former Head of the Department of Fine Arts and Graduate Institute of National Taiwan Normal University

Where will be the future for Chinese ink painting? This is no longer a new and fresh issue. Nonetheless at the time when the psychological anxiety and apprehension are brought by the advent of "millennium"this becomes an old issue no longer provided with satisfactory answer; and it is raised again at the time when it marches into the year 2000. Moreover the unprecedented care and expectation are raised for anyone who strive for brainstorming or maybe it can sort out a comparatively clarifying concept to serve as the continuing research objective upon the arrival of another "millennium".

Lee is the one who lives in the age of anxiety and uncertainty therefore the things that he needs to think about are much more complex. He is the kind of person who is always striving to be the best in studies and also thinks at the same time therefore he has already been not the one who would confine the Chinese ink painting within a one dimensional thinking mode so as to facilitate the interpretation; in addition, as long as one quotes some of the sentences within his listed creative ideas, one would find easily about Lee's anxiety for "the thought could never be careful enough". The following are several quotes to substantiate this statement:

(1) Transformation of ancient and contemporary spirit, exchange between Chinese and western thoughts.
(2) Combining multiculturalism and creating ethnic characteristics.
(3) Reflecting the reality of life, conveying the era witnessed.
(4) Rooted deep down at the life experience, exhibiting the internal feeling and emotion.
(5) Understanding the artistic context, reflecting the historical truth.
(6) Sensing the modern thoughts, exploring the essence of the mind.

From merely the above mentioned six items one can tell that they have already exceeded way beyond what the characteristics which traditional ink painting should embrace. For the "postmodern"generation, the symptom characterizing the end of century is quite evident whereas Lee's creative ideas and his artworks serve as the best proofs available."Intellectual thinking"is used by Lee to allude for the purpose of exploring the mutual dependent relationship between the group and one self within the society norm: the vital rationality within the expression for self-consciousness by human. In the aspect of formality for that piece of artwork, he did use considerably rational arc, square, perpendicular and parallel geometric forms as well as elements with linear configuration, which form into an indifferent screen of "structuralism"that is both close-knit and interlocking. This is exactly the standard norm for "social system". And Lee's speculation in Chinese main body with western application and multiculturalism would render him as the one who would straddle on the boundary between oriental ink painting and western painting.

His writing of "Ideological deification"originates from the feelings that Lee had regarding the disorderly phenomenon at the end of century, Lee prayed that with Chinese culture orthodoxy which had accumulated wisdom lasted thousands of years, he expected this ideological deification would point the way illuminating the enlightenment and salvation. Carved column, symbolizing the orthodoxy of ancient deity thoughts, are surrounded with imagery of climbing and floating dragons and snakes in addition to scenarios similar to the imaging from Buddhist Falun. And these are expressed via western surrealism with proper pacing and deification triggering through elevation angle perspective, no doubt, this painting is a great artwork.

"Standing tall and forever"is fundamentally a logical thinking which collects all orders from this universe into abstract form. The expression and spiritual symbolism have innate orbits which they rely upon just like the operations of the sun and moon. Lee adopts the abstract Expressionism format and uses ink smudges for extension painting, which adopts the cubism structure and symbols of symbolism, exhibited in array throughout: "Ancient and present are continuing to each other, no need to separate between Chinese and foreign".

Lastly, by illustrating a painting of "reflection of civilization", it serves as proper end to this article. This painting was finished while Lee was in the era dominated by technology and he felt deeply about the drastic changes from human living patterns as well as in the value system whereas these changes often counteract against the natural view which eventually causes the loss of significance of civilization. Technology, without the support of civilization, renders humans to cave in to another undeveloped, barbarian period. Lee relies upon the surreal pattern, vocabulary of symbolism, paints a paw of human reaching into the mysterious universe. Thus whether this is a blessing in disguise or catastrophe remained to be seen whereas the warning message is quite evident throughout the painting.

Lee's paintings are rich in ideological and literary contexts. He has the ideology and technique that can transcend the times of ancient and contemporary and manages to show considerable maturity in his artworks whereas suppose he can pioneer with more diversified approaches on the materials used, in time, he would reach the level of masterpiece.

李憶含的靈動水墨思維演化

——曾長生

國立臺灣師範大學藝術評論博士

　　華裔藝術現代化過程中，思維方式的西方化乃是促使藝術完全進入現代化的關鍵因素。觀二十世紀，華裔藝術家以西方為師，以尋求西方文化根源的努力，隨著社會現實的改變而調整前進的腳步，初期學習的是技法，中期是理論，最後是思維方式。如今，大家終於瞭解到，只有技法與理論的模仿，並不足以創作現代藝術，重要的是要瞭解西方現代人如何想像人與其所處的空間和時間之關係，以及那建構自我成為有意義之個體的全套思維模式。

　　傅柯（Michel Foucault, 1926-1984）在他的名作《詞與物》中稱，在十九世紀中葉之前，一般藝術理論的四個領域：再現（representation）理論、表達（articulation）理論、指明（designation）理論、衍生（derivation）理論，支撐著藝術家的思維方式。印象派之後，藝術思維的方式被四個理論所取代，它們是人的有限性（finitude）、經驗與先驗（the empirical and the transcendental）的互証、我思與非思（the cogito and the unthought）、起源與歷史等理論。這四種理論構成了現代思想的基本架構，此認識論上的四邊形，雖看似各自獨立，實則相輔相生。現在我們就來檢視一下李憶含的藝術思維模式演化。

一、人類的有限性

　　在現代思想中，事物被定位在其各自的內在規律內，而人的存在附屬於事物，人的存在與事物產生直接的聯繫。人的存在既然從屬於物，物是有限的，因而人也是有限的。人如同物一樣，有其歷史的起源與終結；人因為勞動、生活、說話，因而人的存在必然不是永恆而超越的，他必定從這些與物的關係才能彰顯出來。人的有限之存在由知識的實證性所預報或彰顯，在現代思想中，人不再是獨立於萬物之外超然之存在，人只是生物之一，其生命是有限的，而且不能逃避生老病死的命運。在藝術與物的這一共存中，通過由再現所揭示的，是否正是現代藝術家的有限性。事實上，在西方文化中，藝術家的存在和造型藝術的存在從未能共存與相互連接，它們的不相容乃是現代思想的基本特徵之一。

　　20世紀以來，人類文明追求的意義是在於尋求一種最樸實歸真的境界，並極富有原創性的人類社會之本然或真相，且促成有益於個體與實現的人文社會發展。藝術家抱持普世性的人文思想進行創作，而產生獨特的表現形式，並以中西合併方式將美學特色予以深化表現。李憶含表示，藝術可以在人的內心深處，也可以在人的生活周遭，藝術的可貴之處就是讓你活出自信，同時藝術也是佛法的化身、宇宙真理的化身，當心靈打開時藝術就在你身邊。

　　李憶含的創作，將水墨作品賦予人文的關懷，探索中國古文明印象及傳統與現代，東方與西方文化中去找尋自我的定位。不斷創新求變，創作時心靈好像一輪明月，李憶含將思想融入在創作的繪畫裡面，讓觀賞的人感覺到他創作的精、氣、神層面。以往一般繪畫追求賞心悅目，只做到了怡情的效果，李憶含認為創作還需要有精神內涵，並且自我鞭策，每一次創作都要超越自我心靈的呈現，他不只是為畫而畫，更是為現今人文、哲學秉持大愛無私的精神，用關懷之情把創作付託新生命一般，源源不絕。

昔日悠然的生命印象與美麗記憶，不但豐富了個人的自然經驗，也體現出自身之人文涵養，使得藝術契合主體的心靈意識。經由「精神性」理念的清楚確立，從中自己更加體認「藝術即道理」，也就是說，既是一種正向、系統的風格發展，也是一種有機、整體之型態趨向，因此，有關人生種種的遷異與變化，包括生活、生存、生命之意識或覺察，除了說明時空更迭和境界轉換，無形中促進了藝術的「質／能」衍義，呈現出真實之「精／神」形象。

二、起源與歷史

　　時間是人類所定出的思考模式之一。物並無記憶，但人類有記憶的本能。人類以自身的經驗建立起物的時間表（年代學），此舉乃是為了自身的利益，為了建構人的記憶之確定性。時間表提供人類思考經驗的過程，但對現代人而言，時間本身並非僅僅是一張平面光滑的圖表而已，它也具有自身的生命，有其起點和終點。事物的起源必得仰賴人的記憶。但因物的起源在宇宙開始時便以存在，以物為中心點，成為建構起源的工具，尋找人的起源已成為現代人的一大問題，亦即，以時間系列建構一個永遠不存在起源點的起源故事，起源永遠只能在思想中存在。因此，其起源永遠處於不確定的狀態。它的不確定性已成為現代人思考上的焦慮來源，這是因為人必須從生命、自然、歷史等，找到認同。

　　經由碩彥明師的指導、學界前輩的引領，以及先進同道的共勉，李憶含除了加深藝術意義之理解與詮釋，在研學、治藝的經驗中，也不斷增廣「美」的見聞和知識；於靜思、內省之體悟裡，持續豐實「好」的精神及內涵。因此，有關西方藝術問題的意識衍異，不會給自己精神導向任何困擾，主要原因在於：將其視為對應「靈動」的直接線索，藉以解明延展「契機」之研究進路；同時，也以「不忘初心」的思想、理念，依「恆常貞定」的情感、情緒，顯見 ＝理應「尊重己靈」，藝術靈動實屬「體中本含」。期望以此個人化創作美學觀，明確東方超現實的風格意涵，釐正當代精神性之圖式象徵。

　　李憶含綜合藝學博思的經驗過程，將相關場合之學術意見，予以概括性的歸納記錄，其中，包含傳統研究的見解與主張，現代探索的思想和論說，乃至當代實驗的觀念及演繹，個人選擇較為印象深刻的，予以簡明列舉於下：如林玉山的「自然生動」、孫家勤的「精神融貫」、鄭善禧的「養正導和」、王哲雄的「古今一氣」、王秀雄的「超現實說」、王友俊的「渾厚溫潤」、江明賢的「創作批評」、何懷碩的「心象風景」、黃光男的「東方意象」，以及羅芳的「當代文人」和劉文潭的「藝術品味」、謝里法的「史實演繹」等等；至於在展覽會場及研討會上，與臺灣學者專家請益和領會，如李奇茂的「突破創新」、高木森的「美與藝論」、曾蕭良的「心靈光譜」、袁金塔的「臺灣主體」、梁秀中的「運筆迴返」、張俊傑的「思和運用」、張隆延的「筆入神出」、董夢梅的「藝術興趣」、傅申的「書藝自然」、傅佑武的「書法構成」、歐豪年的「活化傳統」，甚或劉國松的「水墨與道」等等；此外，與大陸學者專家對話及互動，如汪聞的「書道發展」、皮道堅的「中國基因」、何家英的「理與非理」、沈揆一的「文化認同」、袁運生的「魂兮歸來」、薛永年的「主動的人」、易英的「水墨意義」、夏鑄琦的「傳統精神」、孫景波的「東方之氣」、潘公愷的「文化轉型」，甚或魯虹的「水墨演變」和羅世平的「現代形態」等等。

由此看來，諸多學者專家揭示的藝術見解，確實反映東西遇合之學術觀點，例如：在藝術物質性的形式層面，可謂攸關生存意會與思想光彩；在藝術精神性的內容層面，著實映照生活感通和現實理想；在藝術自然性的意義層面，彷彿顯明生命靈覺及浪漫憧憬。就此而言，無論「體時用中」的藝道美學，抑或「唯證方知」之靈動思惟，隱喻「心和道同」、精神默契，冥合「思與境偕」、氣質隱形，揭顯同時與歷時、物象與心象，以及靈化與活化，儼然如同觀象擬真之「實」與「質」，呼應美學能靜的「隱」和「顯」，契會藝術會動之「抑」及「揚」。

三、經驗與先驗

在現代思想中，人類知識生產決定於形式，但此形式是經驗的真實內容所彰顯的。知識內容的本身即是人做為反思的範圍，其獲得來自一系列對事物的劃分或分割。經驗世界是人判斷事理的基礎，此基礎所建立起的法則又是判斷的客觀標準。在面對實際的經驗分析時，現代藝術家設法把自然的客觀性與通過感覺所勾勒出來的經驗連接起來，亦即把一種文化的歷史與語言連接起來。因此，這種思考方式可以說是藝術家們為了要襯托出個人的經驗與先驗之間的距離，而所做的努力。現代藝術所依賴的造型符號使得經驗與先驗保持分離，但又同時保持相關，這種造型符號在性質上屬於準感覺和準辯證法，其功能在把肉體的經驗和文化的經驗連接起來。

隨著時代、文化、社會的變化，李憶含探尋一種靈動、自然的生命狀態。或許是藝術觀念的選擇、堅持，呈顯的是近乎自由之情境、氛圍，亦是喻為自在的靈性、美感。期望如此擬人化之自然遷異，可以引發浪漫式的精神活動，演繹出自主、超越之藝術創造。在此，李憶含就個人的生命實踐過程，說明有關自我追尋的主體狀態、精神理想的藝術境界，以及藝術探索的風格型態，並就藝術發展的階段性風格，予以簡明分為五個時期：

1、傳統奠基時期（1969-）

此一時期為繪畫初始的階段，在學習的內容上，以傳統水墨概念與西方繪畫知識為主，其中，學習過程是以循序漸進的方式，依照階段次第逐步地推展，以筆墨運用、傳摹臨寫，以及章法佈局之概念為主，從中隱約理解「筋骨血肉」的形質、表象，概略體會「意貫氣足」之神采、真實。

2、自然探秘時期（1979-）

此一時期為大學研究的階段，在學習的內容上，以「寫形狀物」、「探理覓趣」、「搜妙創真」為主，著重媒材技法與情景交融的研究，主要思想在於「外師造化」、「中得心源」與「通體皆靈」，期望藉由「造化之象」的客觀認知，理解「妙合天成」的主觀意趣，從中體會「生機勃發」之精神氣象。

3、人文關懷時期（1997-）

此一時期為碩士研究的階段，在學習的內容上，以「思想溯源」、「古風新貌」、「時代映象」為主，著重形式結構與創意造境之探討，主要藝術思想在於「含真藏古」、「培元固本」與「養正導和」，期望藉由「東方美學」的完整認知，理解「藝術創造」的真正意義，體會「文化自覺」之究竟理想。

4、心靈究竟時期（2006-）

此一時期為博士研究的階段，在學習的內容上，以「靈視意象」、「幻覺形態」、「潛意識流」為主，著重主題內容與觸機神應的探討，主要藝術思想在於「呼喚東方」、「水墨活著」與「靈動叫魂」，期望藉由「玄化秘境」的主觀認知，理解「精神覺照」的終極意旨，體會「靈動自然」之奧妙蘊涵。

5、自有我在時期（2012-）

雖說擬定此一「自有我在」時期，作為個人未來風格研究的階段，其實也是連結過去、延續現在，以及發展未來之研究主軸。這一階段以「變異現象」、「歸元本體」、「顯靈密趣」為主，著重終極意義與自我追尋的探討，主要思想在於「靈動天心」、「覺照人間」和「發明自己」，期望藉由「莊嚴理想」的概念認知，理解「極致現實」的心性意向，體會「清淨本然」之主體狀態。

四、我思與非思

現代思想詢問的是我思如何能處於非思的形式之中，藝術家既要思考造型藝術的存在，又要思考個人生命的存在。這是現代藝術家不同於古典時期藝術思維之處。在古典時期的藝術再現中，藝術家個人生命是隱蔽的，他的存在屈從於他所使用的造型語言之下，在思考再現物的世界時，藝術家與他的非思，是界限分明的。但在現代藝術裡，藝術家總是在創作之際，思考著要如何連接、表明和釋放那些足以表現它個人的存在之語言或概念，換言之，他試圖將他的我思與非思串聯在一起。既要再現物的表象，又要再現藝術家個人的存在，這便是現代藝術家所面臨的問題。

李憶含嘗試以靈動思惟的自主與超越，結合古已有之的觸機和神應，作為東方超現實的藝術演繹觀，以此明證東西方哲學之思想融會，進而依智慧觀照的良知與妙顯，對應精神自覺之主體和心理，演成當代意義性的創作思想論。並且，將有關傳統、現代、當代的藝術型態，予以系統地精神貫通、整合聯繫，以此「靈視、幻象」與潛意識流，探討彩墨超現實畫風的符號、象徵與意涵。使得集象合意的「美」、「妙」之中，呈現出理想的風格呈顯、形式構成，以及技法表現。在此，李憶含以「觸機神應」的延伸思考，概述個人創作實踐之理論依據：

1、觸機神應與變通會適的認知

由《周易·繫辭傳下》「唯變所適」的理解，可知盡心知性能夠彰明客觀世界影響，自是產生迥然不同的心理反應。這種蘊藉奇妙的心理反應，改變了創作者自己的精神意向，也決定了主體對於現實世界的觀點，如同韓康伯注云：「變通貴於適時，趣舍存乎其會。」因此，作為一個主體自覺的藝術家，一個高度思想的創作者，既須清楚「自我本性」與「自然道體」，也要明白「生命精神」和「藝術本質」，源於觸機神應與變通會適的認知，透過精神覺照以「洞性靈之奧區」，從中理解「靈」活「運」用的經驗過程，體會精神理想之象徵與意義。同時，覺察「唯變所適」的思想和觀念，揭顯藝術創造之觀照及思惟；清楚所謂的「精神/自然」，就在於主體的「靈覺/感通」，明白所謂的「藝術/靈動」，就在於自覺的「唯易/思想」。

2、觸機神應與美感意象的覺察

美感除了需要具備主觀審美經驗之外，也需要客觀美學規則的條件。美確實不可能憑空想像，它必須依附於具體物象之上，緣此，藝術之美成為現世生活、精神理想，甚或主體意涵上的折衷與融合，換言之，即

為一種觸機和神應的美感意象。創作者依據自身的歷史、文化與民族等背景，對於有關時代、地域、事件的意識或覺察，與其感官經驗及視覺記憶整合，表達理性、感性和理智之內在體驗，呈現出內心世界的精神狀態。因此，透過觸機神應與美感意象的相互映照，使得藝術意義的對應詮釋、覺性解讀，能夠為鑑賞者意會或感知其旨趣所在，理解其所代表時代意義和文化自覺，從作品的形式及內容來看，也可探悉創作者對於藝術本質的精神體會，此等喻為獨自的內在靈視，誠屬一種自我本性的關懷（thought of the self）。

　　3、觸機神應與興會意義的體會

　　從當代（現代）與當代藝術的探究中，可知由於感官的意識作用和外界相互連繫，在經由不斷延展、重疊及再生的過程中，逐漸形成種種的觀念演繹，擴大認知上的範圍與層面。因此，藉由東西美學思想與哲學理論的研究，理解文化意識中有關感性的直覺（intuition），與理智、理性之間的相互作用。同時，明白東西雙方對於事物的探究，中國傾向於感性直覺與精神體悟，是以心靈覺照的方式體驗真實；西方則著重在客觀理智和科學分析，是以心理感知的方式探究表徵。透過相關資料彙集與梳理，更加體會心的狀態和精神作用，從中清楚感性直覺、明白精神體悟，除了確認主體能動的心性意向，對美的本質之感觀與感受，也有深刻映對的覺察和悟出。基於「本立道生」的心領神會，尋思經由審美活動與藝術創造，演成「會相歸體」之經驗總結，進而釐清東西方藝術的風格和範疇，概述當代藝術之多元化演繹，顯示其中各異其趣的表現特質。

〈主要參考資料〉

（1）王友俊：〈人文的關懷──思源、古風、映象〉

（2）王哲雄：〈李憶含貫串古今兼顧中西的多元文化創作觀〉

（3）袁金塔：〈東方新象‧臺灣本色──談李憶含的水墨創作〉

（4）梁秀中：〈心象為上‧創意表現──談李憶含的藝術取向〉

（5）羅芳：〈茁壯成長──談李憶含〉

（6）顧炳星：〈東方意象‧自然精神──談李憶含現代繪畫風格〉

（7）曾肅良：〈夢的光譜──讀李憶含「繁華緣夢生」系列作品〉

（8）李憶含：《從「靈視、幻象與潛意識流」──探討彩墨超現實畫風的符號、象徵與意涵》

The evolution of the Lee Yi-han's agile water ink thought

Pedro Tseng Ph. D.

In the process of arts modernization for those with Chinese heritage, the westernization of the thinking approach is the key that facilitates the total arts modernization. In view of the twentieth century, artists with Chinese background would serve as apprentice to and learn from the West and strive to seek the source and foundation of western cultures whereas adjust the pace while marching forward along the change of social reality. In the early phase, they learned the technique, in the interim, theory, lastly, the thought approach. As of now, all of us finally realize that only imitation of the technique and theory is not enough for creating modern arts; the important thing is to understand how the modern westerners think as well as their perceived relation between the space and time where they are positioned; in addition, the total set of thinking mode of meaningful individual achieved through self construction.

Michael Foucault (1926-1984) claimed in his masterpiece- "Les Mots et les choses", prior mid 19th century, the four domains of general arts theories were: the representation, the articulation, the designation and the derivation, and they served as the foundation for artist's thought mode. After the age of impressionism, the approach of artistic thought would be replaced by these four theories, i.e. the theories of finitude, the mutual certifications between the empirical and transcendental theories, the cogito and the unthought, origin and history, etc. These four theories constituted the basic tenet of modern thought and the quadrilaterals of the epistemology seemed to be mutually independent whereas in reality, they were complimentary to each other. Now let's review the artistic thought evolution of Lee Yi-han.

I. Human finitude

In modern thought, thing is positioned within respectively internal laws whereas the human existence is affiliated to thing therefore the human existence produces direct connection with thing. Since human existence is affiliated to thing and thing is finite therefore human is also finite. Human, just like thing, has the origin and finality of his history; and human can labor, live and speak therefore the human existence is not necessarily eternal and transcendental and he must demonstrate this through relating these with thing. And the limited human existence can be forecast or highlighted due to empirical knowledge. Hence from the perspective of modern thought, human is no longer independent from all things and has a transcendental existence. Human is one of all living creatures with limited life span in addition to unable to escape from the destiny of living, aging, sickness and death. Amid the coexistence between arts and things, and it reveals through the representation, one would wonder whether this is the finitude of modern artists. In actuality, from the context of western culture, the existence of artist and that of visual arts never can coexist nor interconnect and their incompatibility is one of the characteristics for modern thought.

Since 20th century, the significance of human seeking the civilization rests at looking for a kind of state characterized by the most guileless simplicity in addition to authenticity or truth of human society which is rich in originality. Moreover, it also facilitates the human society development beneficial to individual entity and its realization. Artists, with universally humanistic thinking, proceeds to creative artworks whereas they produce an unique expression format in addition that they add depth to the performance of aesthetics characteristics through combined Sino and western forms. Lee indicates that arts can reside deep down in the human hearts and also around the lives of people. The values of arts exemplify through allowing you with confidence through living and at the same time, arts are also the incarnations of Buddhist and the truth of the universe; thereby when one opens his mind then the arts is right next to you.

In Lee's creative works, the water ink artworks are imbued with humanistic care so as to explore the image of ancient Chinese civilization as well as those of the traditional and modern ages; these artworks seek self-orientation from the oriental and occidental cultures. While constantly seeking for changes, the mind of creation resembles a bright moon. Lee manages to have the thoughts immersed into the paintings of creation allowing the viewing audience to feel the levels of spirit, chi and the verve in his artworks. In the past, general paintings would seek for the state of feast for the eyes which only achieves the pleasing effect whereas Lee recognizes that creation also requires the spiritual content in addition to self-encouragement. Every creation shall transcend the layer of self-consciousness. Lee not only paints for the sake of painting, but also treats it as the spirit of selfless love held by nowadays humanity and philosophy. Lee imbues a new life to his artworks through caring and he never stops.

Life images and beautiful memories of the old days not only enrich individual natural experiences but also realize the self humanistic richness which enables the arts to match to the mind's conscience of the main body. Through the lucid establishment of "spiritual"idea, one can realize "arts is the Way (Tao)"even more from oneself, i.e. it is a positively and systematically stylistic development but also a kind of organic and comprehensive pattern trending; therefore any life differences and changes, including the consciousness and awareness of living, existence and life itself, not only illustrating the time space conversions and the changes of state, virtually promoting the derivation of arts "essence/energy"and displaying the true image of "spirit/mind".

II. Origin and History

Time is one of the thinking modes defined by human. The thing has no memory whereas human has the instinct of memory. Human self-experience is used to establish the time table of thing (geochronology), the act itself is to serve self interest in order to construct the certainty of human memory. Time table provides the process of human thinking experience whereas as far as modern people are concerned, time itself is not only a piece of smooth-plane diagram; it has its life cycle with starting point and the ending. Origin of thing must rely upon human memory; nonetheless since origin of thing exists at the beginning of the universe thereby the thing serves as the center so as to become the tool for constructing the origin. And the origin of the seeker has already become a major issue for modern people, i.e. an origin story using the time series to construct a never existed origin; hence the origin will always exist in the thinking process. Therefore, its origin always exists in an uncertain state. Its uncertainty has become the anxiety source in the thinking process of modern people; and this is because that people must find recognition from life, nature and history, etc.

Due to the guidance provided by masters and renowned teachers, led by senior scholars as well as mutual encouragements from the advanced fellow painters, Lee not only deepens his understanding and interpretation of the artistic significances, but also in his studying and honing his skill experiences, he constantly increases and expands the experiences and knowledge regarding "aesthetics". From the realization from meditation and self-reflection, he continues to enrich the "worthy"spirit and content. Thereby any awareness derivation concerning western arts would not bother him, especially in the aspect of self-spiritual orientation and the prime reason is because that: it is treated as the direct trace corresponding to "agility"which is used to elucidate and extend the study inroad for "moment". At the same time, bearing the thinking and idea of "never forgetting the original intention", following the emotion and intention of "constancy and true to oneself", it would be apparent that the spirit would be natural to "respect one's self-soul"whereas the arts agility is really belonged to "within the body and self-containing". So it is expected that through the individualized creation aesthetics, one can crystallize the stylistic content of oriental surrealism and correct the diagram symbolism of contemporary spirit.

Lee's synthesizes the experience process of the broad thinking in arts and he generally summarizes and records related scholar opinions at appropriate gatherings. Within them, those include the opinion and advocate about traditional research, modern exploration concerning the thinking and exposition and argument, even concept and interpretation of contemporary experiments. I personally select some of the impressive ones and briefly list them as follow: Lin Yu-shan's "naturally vivid", Suen Jia-chin's "spiritually coherent", Zhen Shan-xi's "fostering the properness and guiding to harmony", Wang Jhe-syong's "unchanged throughout the time", Wang Hsiu-hsiung's "surreal postulation", Wang You-jyun's "deep and warm", Chiang Ming shyan's "creative work and critique", Ho Huai-shuo's "image of the mind and scenery", Huang Kuang-nan's "oriental image"and Lo Fong's "contemporary writer"and Liu Wen-tan's "artistic taste"and Hsieh Li-fa's "historical fact interpretation", etc. As for Lee's learning and understanding from Taiwan scholars and experts at expositions and seminars, they are Lee Chi-mao's "breakthrough and innovation", Gao Mu-Sen's "aesthetics and arts theory", Tseng Su-liang's "mind's spectrum", Yuan Chin-taa's "Taiwan main body", Liang Shiow-chung's "return of the technique of using chinese brush and ink", Chun-Chieh chang's "thinking and operation", Chang Long-yien's "writing inspired by holy spirit ",

Guon Muon-mei's "artistic interest", Fu Shen's "naturalness of penmanship", Fu You-wu's "penmanship's construct"and Ou Hao-nian's "revitalized tradition"and even Liu Kuo-Sung's "water ink and the path", etc. Other than these, Lee conducts dialogues and interacts with mainland scholars and experts such as Wuan Wen's "development of calligraphy", Pi Dao-jian's "Chinese genes", Herr Jia-yin's "rational and irrational", Shen Kuiyi's "culture identification", Yuan Yun-sheng's "return of the spirit", Xue Yong-Nian "proactive people", Yi Yin's "water ink significance", Xia Zhu Qi's "Traditional spirit", Pan Gongkai's "cultural transformation"and even Lu Hong's "water ink evolution"and Luo Shi-pin's "modern forms", etc.

In view of this, artistic views revealed by many scholars and experts indeed reflect the scholarly view of fortuity of the east and west; for instance: the formality level of artistic materialism can be referred as concerning the survival perception and ideological brilliance; at the content level of artistic spirituality, it indeed reflects the living sense and realistic ideal; at the significance level of artistic naturalness, it seems to highlight the life soul perception as well as romantic longing. As far as these are concerned, no matter whether be it as the arts aesthetics of "timely middle of the road approach"or agile thinking of "knowing only through verification", the metaphor of "identical mind and Tao", spiritual teamwork, combined offerings of "thinking and state", invisible temperament, revealing both instantaneously and lasting, phenomena and mental imagery, spiritualization and activation, they are just like the "actuality"and "texture"corresponding to the "hidden"and "revealing"of aesthetics which can be static and matching to the "curbing"and "rising"of the arts which can be moving.

III. Experience and transcendence

In modern thinking, the production of human knowledge is predicated on the form whereas this form is evident through the true content of experience. The content of knowledge itself is the scope of human reflection and the acquiring of it originates from a series of division and separation from things. The world of experience is the foundation for human making judgments toward things and the rule of establishment of this foundation is the objective standard for judgment. While analyzing experience when confronting the reality, modern artist tries to connect the experiences from natural objectivity with those described through sensory, i.e. connecting the history and language of a certain culture. Hence this thinking mode can be said as that the artists try to set off the distance between personal experience and the transcendence, the efforts being made. Modeling notation relied upon by modern artists enables the separation between experience and transcendence and simultaneously maintains relevance. And this modeling notation is attributed as quasi feeling and dialectics in nature and its function aims to connect the physical and cultural experiences.

Along with changes stemmed from the times, cultures and societies, Lee explores a kind of life state characterized by intelligence and nature. Or maybe they are choices and persistence of artistic ideas and what are displayed are scenarios and atmospheres that are nearly free, i.e. they are metaphors of free spirituality and aesthetics. With expectations of such personified natural migration, it can trigger romantic spiritual activity and derive an autonomous and surpassing artistic creation. At this, Lee illustrates artistic state concerning self-seeking main state and spiritual ideal as well as artistic exploration of stylistic pattern in addition that they can be simply divided into 5 phases as far as the periodic style of artistic development is concerned:

1、Traditional and laying-the-foundation period (1969-)

In this period, it was the preliminary phase for painting. In the contents of learning, they were primarily traditional water ink concepts and western painting knowledge. In it, the learning process was conducted in a progressive way and proceeding according to phases so as to expand and primarily concerning concepts of the technique of using Chinese brush to draw lines and how to use ink, copying and sketching, methodicalness and layout. From them, Lee could faintly comprehend the form and quality and the appearance of "the bones and fleshes"approximately realize the vividness and truth of "significance and literary ambience".

2、Nature exploration period (1979-)

In this period, it was characterized by university research. As for learning content, they were primarily in the "sketching the form and of all creatures", "exploring the nature truth and seeking pleasure"and "seeking the wonder and creating the original"which focused on media technique as well as studied the scenes. Main thoughts were residing at "taught by external", "acquired in heart"and "spirit throughout the body". It was expected that by the objective cognition of "phenomena of creation", he could understand the subjective pleasure and significance of "naturalness"so as to realize the spiritual atmosphere of "robustness".

3、Humanistic care period (1997-)

At this period, it was Lee's research during his master program. In the learning content, they were primarily of "tracing back to the origin of thought", "new look of ancient style"and "times image"which focused on the exploring form structure and creation of situation. And the primary artistic thinking were of "truth within hidden ancient", "cultivating and solidifying the foundation"as well as "raising the proper and directing to harmony"with an expectation that Lee could realize the ideal of "cultural awareness"through comprehensive cognition of "oriental aesthetics"and understand the true significance of "arts creation".

4、Mind and soul searching period (2006-)

In this period, Lee was at the stage of doctoral research. As for learning content, it was primarily of "the image of spiritual vision", "form of hallucination"and "subconscious style"which focused on exploration of subject content and opportunity and reaction. His primary artistic thinking was of "calling the orient", "living water ink"and "agile soul searching"with an expectation that by subjective recognition of "mystifying the uncharted"so that Lee could understand the ultimate significance of "spiritual reawakening"and realize the secret of "agile and natural".

5、Self-owning and self-present period (2012-)

Although planning this self-owning and self-present period as the phase for individual futuristic style research, in actuality, this was also a research main theme meant to connect the past and extend the present as well as develop the future. In this phase, "variation", "return back to the Noumenon "and "manifestation and secret interest"were the primary concern which focused on the exploration of ultimate significance and self-pursuit. Main thought rested at "agile the heart of heaven", "self-reflection shining on earth"and "inventing oneself"with the expectation to understand the orientation of "ultimate reality"and realized the main state of "cleanness and naturalness"through the concept recognition of "solemn ideal".

IV: The cogito and the unthought

What modern thinking asks is that how the cognito can exist in the form of unthought. Artist not only wants to think about the existence of visual arts but also think about the existence of individual life. This is exactly the artistic thinking of the modern artist differing that of classic period. In the reproduction of arts during classic era, the individual life of artist is hidden and his existence is subservient to the modeling language that he uses. While in the world of thought the reproduction entity, there is a clear delineation of boundary between the artist and his unthought whereas in modern arts, the artist is always thinking about how to connect, express clearly and release those language and concept that can adequately express his individual existence. Alternatively he tries to connect the cogito with unthought. So not only the superficial phenomenon of reproduction material is wanted but also the individual existence of the reproduction artist and this is the problem that confronts the modern artist.

Lee tries to integrate the ever existing touch opportunity and heavenly response based upon the autonomy and transcendence of agile thinking to serve as the artistic interpretation concept so as to verify the thinking merging east and west philosophies. Moreover, according to the consciousness and emergence of wisdom, corresponding to the Noumenon and mindset of spiritual self-awareness, he can derive the creative thinking theorem with contemporary significance. In addition, he systematically and spiritually connects and consolidates all relating to traditional, modern and contemporary artistic patterns. He applies the "spiritual vision and illusion"and sub consciousness to explore the signs, symbols and significances of color ink surrealism. And these enable the images within the context of "beauty"and "wonder", exhibiting ideal style, the construction of form as well as the technique. At there, Lee generally describes his personal creation and implementation theory foundation through the extended thinking of "touch opportunity and heavenly response".

1、 Cognition of touch opportunity-heavenly response and workaround to fit

From the understanding of "only change will fit"in "Zhou Yi. Shi Tse Chuan Part II"one can learn that trying one's best with knowing the nature can illustrate the impact by external world; and this would create totally different psychological response. This kind of psychological response breeding wonder can change the author's spiritual orientation and also determine the Noumenon viewpoints toward reality world. Just like Han Kon-ber noted: "Timely change is most precious, choice exists only needed". Hence, to be an artist of self-awareness in the Noumenon, a highly thinking creator, one must understand "self-nature"and "natural path"but also the "spirit of life"and "artistic nature"and these are all originated from the cognition of touch-opportunity and heavenly response and change-will-fit. Through spiritual awareness with "penetrating the mystic area of the soul"one can understand the experience process of "agile"and "apply"and realize the symbol and significance of spiritual ideal. At the same token, be aware of the thinking and idea of "only change will fit"which reveals the contemplation and thinking of artistic creation. If one understands the so called "spirit/nature"which resides at the Noumenon's "perception/feeling"then one would understand the so called "arts/agility"which is exactly the self-aware "only Yi/thought".

2、 The notice of touch opportunity and heavenly response and beauty image

Beauty image not only requires possessing subjective aesthetics experience, but also conditions for objective aesthetics rules. Beauty indeed cannot be dreamt up and it must be attached to some concrete object. Because of this, the beauty of arts becomes part of life and spiritual ideal and even including maybe comprise and fusion of the Noumenon significance. In another words, it is a kind of aesthetics image of touch-opportunity and heavenly response. The creative artist, according to his own backgrounds like history, culture and ethnicity, and the consciousness or awareness concerning the era, physical location and incident in addition to the integration of his sensory experience and visual memory, represents inner rational, emotional and intellectual experience, exhibits the spiritual state of inner world. Thereby, through the mutual reflection between touch-opportunity and heavenly response and aesthetics image, it enables the corresponding interpretation and the feel of this interpretation for artistic significance to allow the viewer to sense or perceive where the purpose lies at, understand the times significance and cultural awareness which it represents. From the perspective of artwork form and content, one can also explore the author's artistic nature and spiritual realization and all of these can be the metaphor for independent inner clairvoyant and it is really a kind thought of the self.

3、 The experience of the touch-opportunity and heavenly response and pleasingly meeting significance

From the explorations on this era (modern) and contemporary arts, one can be aware of the mutual connection between sensory consciousness and external events, and through the process of constantly extending, overlapping and regenerating, it gradually forms multiple conceptual evolutions and expands the scope and layer of cognition. Thereby through research on oriental and occidental aesthetics thinking and philosophical theory, one can understand the mutual interaction between cultural consciousness's related sensory intuition, sensibility and rationality. In the mean time, one can understand the exploration of the matters perceived by both orient and occident whereas China tends to lean toward sensory intuition and spiritual realization and experience the truth through the approach of sensing by the mind and soul whereas the west tends to focus on objective rationale and scientific analysis and explore the characterization via psychological perception. And through the compilation and organization of related information, one can even more realize the state of mind and spiritual function and can clearly sense the intuition, understand the spiritual realization. Besides affirming the actively moving mind intention, one can also deeply reflect on the awareness and realization from sensing and feeling the essence of beauty. Based upon the implicit understanding of "establishing the foundation and creation of the path", one can think about the summary of experience for deriving "all images converged to the Noumenon"through thinking about the aesthetic activity and artistic creativity so as to further clarify the style and the scope of east and west arts, generally describe the diversified interpretation of contemporary arts, display different styled performance characteristics.

⟨Major reference materials⟩

(1) Wang You-jyun: "Humane care - the source, antiquity, image."

(2)Wang Jhe-syong: "The diversified cultural creative concept that connect throughout ancient and nowadays covering both Sino and the west by Lee Yi-han."

(3) Yuan Chin-taa: "New image of the orient. True color of Taiwan—Let's talk about the water ink creation by Lee Yi-han. "

(4) Liang Shiow-chung: " Mind image tops all. Creative performance—Let's talk about the artistic orientation of Lee Yi-han."

(5)Lo Fong: " Thriving—Let's talk about Lee Yi-han. "

(6) Gu Bing-sing: "Oriental image. Spirit of nature—Let's talk about Lee Yi-han's modern painting style."

(7) Tseng Su-liang: "Spectrum of the dream—Reading about the series of artwork 'Bustling dream' by Lee Yi-han. "

(8) Lee Yi-han: *Exploration of the signs, symbols and significance of color ink surrealism painting style from "Spiritual vision, illusion and the unconsciousness."*

為時代歷史寫下輝煌的一頁　｜　王友俊　國立臺灣師範大學美術研究所教授

　　在其兢兢業業的努力中，繪畫思想有了極大的變化，探究表現的方向亦時有突破，實在是一段極其可貴的創作歷程。整體看來，憶含在這短短的一兩年中，即能超越自己對繪畫藝術原有的認知，而有今日這些有思想有旨趣相當感人的製作，實在是一件令人欽佩的事，期待他繼續努力，百尺竿頭更進一步，為自己、為民族、為時代、為歷史寫下輝煌的一頁。

在現代水墨上的求新求變　｜　吳心荷　國立彰化師範大學美術研究所教授

　　憶含的畫中有一份思古的幽情、宇宙穹蒼的浩瀚情懷和東方哲學的冥思，對水墨氣韻的營造，嘗試運用各種不同的表現方法，並力求畫面構成的多樣性，都說明了憶含在現代水墨創作上求新求變的決心。現代水墨的創作正值方興未艾的滔段，邁向21世紀更企盼更多的畫壇新秀注入新的氣象，使其更加蓬勃發展，相信憶含必是其中的一顆明星。

為現代水墨注入新生命　｜　李振明　前國立臺灣師範大學藝術學院院長

　　藝術貴乎創造，此不論中西繪畫均當如是。李憶含之現代水墨創作，從觀照自然之寫生入手，而能於師造化之外另闢蹊徑，善用傳統書法性線條之外的另類「新筆墨」嘗試。且不排它地與固有技法相融相生，開拓了水墨的新領域。豐富的形式中，亦蘊涵著深刻的環境互動與人文關懷。個人獨特的造形語彙，以不譁眾的真誠探討，配合多面向的題材選用，為現代水墨注入一新的生命力。

維繫東方藝術固有特色　｜　林仁傑　國立臺灣師範大學美術研究所教授

　　在藝術領域裡，傳統審美標準一直掌控藝術創作與藝術鑑賞的思維準則，導致創作者與觀賞者自我思辨能力的弱化。後現代西方藝術現象的最大優點，就在於喚起創作與觀賞的自我思辨能力。李憶含先生的藝術創作正足以說明東方後現代藝術表現也已展現這股效能。最可貴的是：他在解構與再建構的過程中，依然透過人文關懷固執地維繫東方藝術的固有特色。

為現代水墨畫壇揭櫫一新的方向　　｜　袁金塔　國立臺灣師範大學美術研究所教授

　　觀憶含的畫，讓我覺得自己彷彿是個「夜行者」。在無邊無際的蒼穹中馳騁，如夢似真，那兒有宇宙的神祕，有人文的哲思，有生命的真情。以「入古尋新」、「古法今用」的繪畫理念，融匯源自本土新觀念、新思維，呈現具東方精神、當代意涵的臺灣水墨新風貌，並具有文學內容與哲學思想，為現代水墨畫壇揭櫫一新的方向。

哲學思想、耐人尋味　　｜　孫家勤　國立臺灣師範大學美術研究所教授

　　人生哲學隨著年齡方能加深認識，影響著繪畫的內涵，是畫家成長的重要因素，這就是我國傳統所謂藝術家需要多讀書的道理。憶含弟近日的作品，對人生哲學有著深入的思考與探討，他將繪畫無痕跡的帶入哲學思想的境界，充實的畫面內容，使其作品不止是美的追求，而有咀嚼不盡的回味，耐人深思，喜而識之。

入古尋新、古法今用　　｜　梁秀中　前國立臺灣師範大學藝術學院院長

　　他以「入古尋新」、「古法今用」的理念，為使現代水墨畫有更新的創意。其中有六幅給我印象最深：〈菩提心木〉、〈自由心證〉、〈中觀思想〉、〈本立道生〉、〈古道夢迴〉及〈無華之華〉，這些作品從畫題中就可知道這次研究的主題——人文關懷。而且他更從文史哲學的思源中去探究，也從歷覽古中國文明印象中及傳統與現代、東方與西方文化中去找尋自我的定位。

觀照自然、體悟人生　　｜　傅佑武　前國立臺灣師範大學美術系主任

　　藝術的表現，包含美的意味與真、善的成分。在現實時空下的反映人類的思想和情感，使得其呈現多元的複雜變化，然真誠的藝術創作者本身應具備時代意識、思想呈現的能力與傾向，更須有關懷社會、省思自然與人文的精神特質。李憶含近作風格富有哲學意涵，畫面構成採象徵、超現實等表現手法，從觀照自然、體悟人生到自我思維轉化形成主體性創作精神，極為可貴。

心靈如大圓鏡智觀照出華麗世界

曾肅良　國立臺灣師範大學美術研究所教授

　　從玄學的角度來看，他所刻意營造的晶瑩剔透的效果，和半抽象或半具像的表現，恰如其分地，呈顯出他對內在性靈的體悟。我彷彿看到一顆純真原始的心靈，一如一面透光的明鏡（佛家以「大圓鏡智」象徵最高智慧），可以映照出外界的萬事萬物，從畫作裡，我直覺地感受到他的心靈，正隨著年齡的增長與領會，緩緩地沉澱，悠悠地息止，他的心靈似乎已經質變成一顆晶亮圓融、具有那份心靈的能力的多面體，當面對紛繁的人間萬象，絲毫不被染污，而且反射出如萬花筒般的華麗外界。

準確掌握藝術創作方向

羅芳　二十一世紀中國現代水墨畫會會長

　　繪畫追求賞心悅目，只做到了怡情的效果，要能代表文化的一環，還需要有精神內涵，每個人的思想，則是內涵不可或缺的主導，我們樂見臺灣師大美術研究所培養了一群會思考的藝術工作者，也許不夠成熟，但是他們的確掌握了藝術創作的方向，李憶含尤其是其中的佼佼者，在二年短短的時間中，能找到了自我表現和透通人生哲理的思維，確立應追求的方向，他對空間的處理，細膩的手法，揭櫫新的探求理念，相信這是正確的方向。

"Agility"and "operation" —— Exaltation and reverberation

Wang You-jyun   Professor at Institute of Fine Arts, National Taiwan Normal University

Amid the striving in all painters' works, the thought of painting has undergone tremendous changes whereas the direction in exploring the expression methods would occasionally manage to have certain breakthrough; and these are periods with admirable creative journeys. In summary, Lee had well exceeded his own original recognition on the painting arts during a rather short period of 1 to 2 years. Up till now, these work pieces immersed in thoughts, with objective in mind and also rather touching, have become something rather commendable. We all expect that he can continue what he has been doing and go further beyond, whether just for himself, for the peoples, for the times and even history, he can turn all of these into a new page.

Wu Hsin-ho   Professor at Institute of Fine Arts, National Changhua Normal University

Lee's paintings are rich with a sense of missing the times past, feelings of the vast expanse of the universe as well as meditation characterizing oriental philosophy. The honing for ink spirit in his painting underwent several different expression changes and his striving for multiplicity in the painting configuration underscores his determination for constant tryouts and changes in ink painting creation. Contemporary ink painting is at the turbulent crossroad of changes; while marching into the 21st century, the expectation resides at wishing more of the infusions by rookie painters would be forthcoming; eventually these would render the prosperity in development. And we believe Lee would undoubtedly be one of the shining stars.

Lee Jhen-ming   Former president of College of Arts, National Taiwan Normal University

Arts is esteemed at the process of creation; no matter whether be it Chinese or western painting. Lee's contemporary ink painting makes its entry via contemplation of natural painting whereas he creates another path into arts by mimicking the great nature. And he is good at applying the untraditional "new pen stroke" beyond the confines by traditional calligraphy lines. And his approach does not expel other existing techniques instead, he manages to blend in all their strengths and have them coexisted harmoniously thereby Lee pioneers into a brand new territory for ink painting. Amid these rich formalities, there are imbedded with in-depth environmental interactions and humanity. His personal unique creative vocabulary, making truthful exploration without worrying about pleasing the crowd, manages to work in conjunction with multifaceted selection of topics; ultimately, Lee injects a set of new life force into the contemporary ink painting.

Lin Jen-Chien   Professor at Institute of Fine Arts, National Taiwan Normal University

In the domain of arts, traditional standard of aesthetics has always in control of the thought principle for arts creation and appreciation, which cause the weakening in the ability of self-criticism and thinking for both the creators and viewers alike. The greatest advantage for the phenomenon of post-modern Western arts is at the ability to reawaken the ability of self-criticism for creators and viewers. Lee's arts creation is the right vehicle to elucidate why oriental post-modern arts expression has already exhibited this kind of momentum. Most precious of all: Amid the process of deconstruction and reconstruction, Lee still obstinately maintains the inherent characteristics of Oriental Art through his concerns and cares for humanity.

Yuan Chin-taa   Professor at Institute of Fine Arts, National Taiwan Normal University

Viewing Lee's painting, it allows me to fancy myself as "nightcrawler". Riding under the dome of boundless sky, in a surreally dreamy state, where it has the mystery of the universe and also philosophical thoughts of humanity in addition to life's truthfulness. Lee applies the painting ideas like "seeking for new amid the ancient"and "new application of the ancient method", he manages to infuse and integrate new ideas and new thoughts originated from native lands, to exhibit a new outlook of Taiwan ink painting possessing oriental spirit as well as contemporary significance. They also possess literary contents as well as philosophical thoughts and point to a new direction for contemporary ink painting.

Suen Jia-chin   Professor at Institute of Fine Arts, National Taiwan Normal University

The knowledge if one's philosophy in life only deepens along with the aging process which would impact the contents of painting and is also the vital element for the growth of any painter. This is exactly the reason why the so called artists attributed by our tradition need to study more. Lee's recent artworks project an in-depth thinking and exploration aspect toward philosophy in life and Lee manages to elevate the paintings into the realm of philosophical thoughts without leaving any trace behind, it enriches the contents of the painting, rendering his artwork no longer confined to the mere pursuit of aesthetics, but also leaves behind a sweet aftertaste after endless chewing; it is both thought provoking and loving it once one gets to know.

Liang Shiow-chung   Former president of College of Arts, National Taiwan Normal University

Lee applies the ideas of "seeking the new among the ancient"and "contemporary application for the ancient method"to render the contemporary ink painting with even more fresh creativity. In them, there are 6 paintings left an indelible impression in my mind: "Wooden core of Bodhi". "Discretional evaluation of evidence", "Meso thoughts", "Way(Tao) arises from the solid fundamentals", "Dream escape in the ancient path"and "minimalist Hua". From the topics of these painting, one can learn about the subjects of this research—Humanity and caring. Moreover Lee explores from the perspective of fountainheads of literary, history and philosophy and also seeks for self-positioning from the overviews made in the ancient Chinese civilization images as well as traditional, modern, oriental and occidental cultures.

| **Fu You-wu**   Former Head of Department of Fine Arts, National Taiwan Normal University

Performance of arts is comprised of aesthetics significance and components in truth and goodness. Under the dome of temporal reality, it reflects the thinking and emotion of human which renders them in exhibiting a complex and diverse change whereas the creator of sincere and truthful artworks, he himself should possess the faculty and inclination of era consciousness and thought presenting capability, he needs to have the spiritual quality of caring for the society and reflections upon both the nature and humanity. Recent styles in the works by Lee are rich with philosophical contents, and the painting configuration adopts the expression techniques of symbolism and surrealism thereby it transforms itself into subjectively creative spirit from observing the great nature, life realization and self-thinking status. This, by itself, is quite a feat.

| **Tseng Su-liang**   Professor at Institute of Fine Arts, National Taiwan Normal University

From the vantage point of metaphysics, the sparking and crystal-clear effect which Lee deliberately hones and the performance characterized by semi-abstract or semi-figurative, aptly, showcase his realization of his inner mind and soul. It seems like I had seen a true and original heart and mind and just like a one-side translucent mirror ("Da Yuan Jin Zhe"is the symbol used by Buddhist as the wisdom of highest order). It can then reflect all things externally. And from his painting artworks, I can instinctively feel what his heart and mind perceives. Along with aging and realization, slowly it precipitates, gradually and peacefully it stops. His mind and soul seem to already transform into a polyhedron of bright harmony with a share of ability of mind. While confronting numerous human Vientiane, it will not be polluted at all, instead, it reflects just like kaleidoscope-like magnificent outside world.

| **Lo Fong**   Chairman. 21st century Chinese modern ink painting association

If the painting only seeks for the pleasing to the eyes, it only achieves the purpose of cheering at best. Suppose it wants to represent a part of culture, then it requires spiritual contents whereas everyone's thinking is an indispensible guidance and we are pleased to witness Institute of Fine Arts, NTNU, who has cultivated a group of thinking arts workers. May be they are not matured enough but they indeed control the direction for arts creation and Lee, among them, managed to locate the self-expression within a short span of two years, and though his thinking in the philosophy of life, he established the direction where he supposed to follow. His processing on space, his delicate technique, reveals a brand new way in exploring ideas; I believe this is the right direction for further pursuit.

不把水墨性格侷限於物質性思維，而是以明確的精神性
覺照，在具有高度文化理念中，將中國傳統水墨精華萃
取、凝聚，並且經由完整的審視、重探，朝向現代（當
代）藝術的轉變、化成，明證古今本相續的理想旨趣，應
驗中外何需分之現實義理。——李憶含

楊枝源 攝

靈視・幻象

——當代水墨作品欣賞

信陽光照 - 千年豔

Faith in sunlight - Eternally gorgeous

2017　紙本設色　246×123cm

早春迷濛 - 幾多紅
Early spring mist - Wonderfully red
2017　紙本設色　246×123cm

早春迷濛 - 幾多紅｜局部
Early spring mist - Wonderfully red｜detail

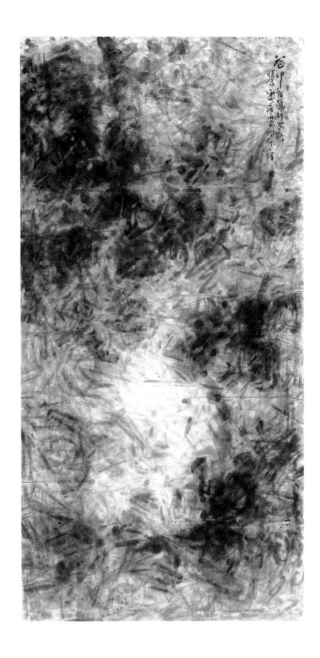

太素元清 · 極精義

Grand elements · Refined meaning

2017　紙本設色　246×123cm

花中有道 · 微密契

Way through the flowers · Mysticism

2017　紙本設色　246×123cm

寒雨詩興 - 寧波行
Poetry in the cold rain - Trip to Ningpo
2017　紙本設色　246×123cm

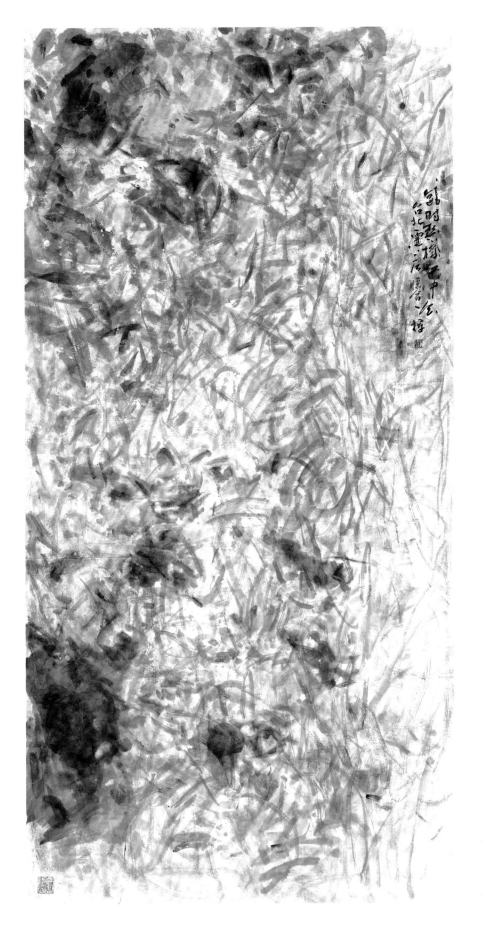

感時契機‧興中會
Opportunities of sensation
- China Restoration Society
2017　紙本設色　246×123cm

徵明幽靜 - 含真蘊

Zhengming tranquility - With truth

2017　紙本設色　246×123cm

游心顯性 - 嚮於消

Playful heart personality - Yearning for solitude

2017　紙本設色　246×123cm

湛寂虛靈 - 無盡藏
Lonely and empty spirits - Endless Treasures
2017　紙本設色　246×123cm

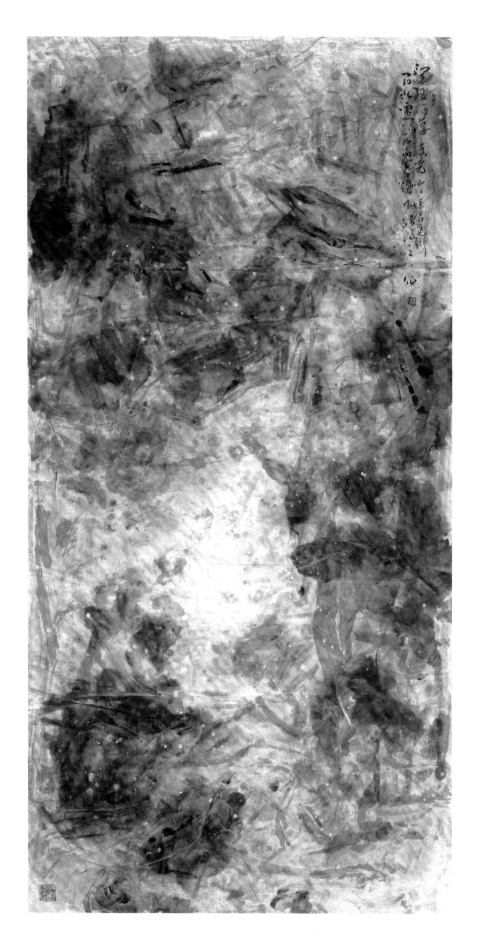

望極河漢 - 流光吟
Galaxy gazing - Streamer recitation
2017　紙本設色　246×123cm

何日重遊
When to revisit
2016 紙本設色 177×95cm

春秋鳥來（局部）
Wulai in spring and autumn times（detail）

春秋烏來
Wulai in spring and autumn times
2016　紙本設色　177×95cm

寂寞行路

Lonely travels

2016　紙本設色　177×95cm

西府海棠

Kaido crabapple

2016　紙本設色　143×76cm

寧波散心
Taking a stroll in Ningpo
2016　紙本設色　143×76cm

罔極化境
Boundless parental care
2016　紙本設色　137×69cm

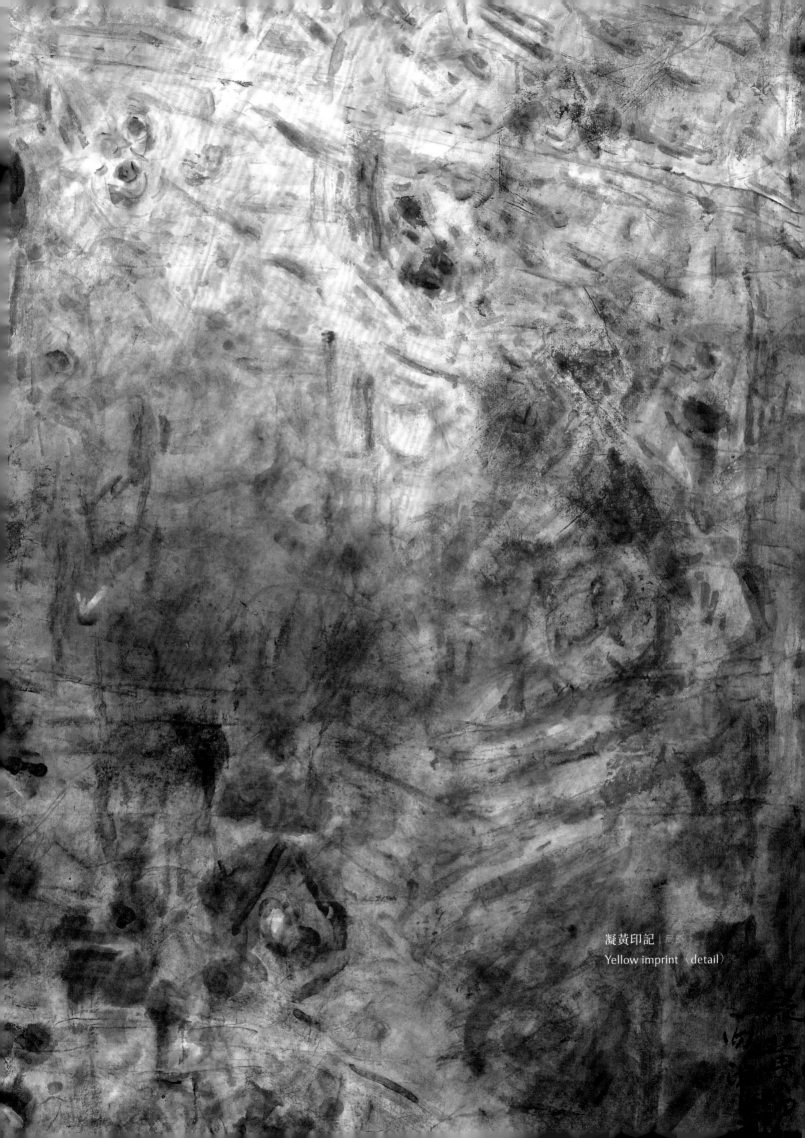

凝黃印記 | 局部
Yellow imprint（detail）

凝黃印記

Yellow imprint

2016 紙本設色 143×76cm

無言海域

Speechless sea

2016 紙本設色 143×76cm

幾多春紅
How red is the spring
2016 紙本設色 143×76cm

石花可人
Adorable stone flowers
2016 紙本設色 137×69cm

解夢花語

Dream interpretations and floral language

2016　紙本設色　137×69cm

東方勁紅

Oriental red

2016　紙本設色　68×23cm

零度臘梅

Wintersweet in the freezing cold

2016 紙本設色 68×22cm

綠衣黃裡

Green clothes with yellow lining

2016 紙本設色 68×20cm

綠衣黃裡 | 局部
Green clothes with yellow lining〈detail〉

藝道美學・靈動思惟

相如賦歸
Xiangru homeward bound
2016　紙本設色　45×69cm

剎那非遠

The moment is close at hand

2016 紙本設色 76×76cm

使信子云

Messenger's words

2016　紙本設色　76×76cm

綺麗珊瑚
Beautiful coral
2016　紙本設色　76×76cm

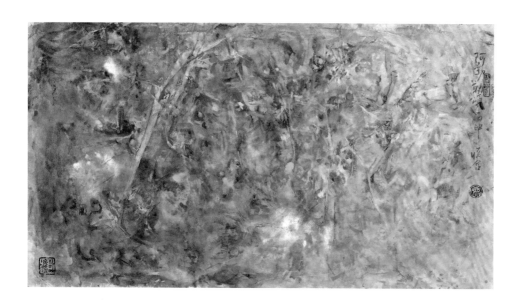

阿勃勒頌
Eulogizing the golden shower tree
2016　紙本設色　38×68.5cm

阿勃勒頌｜局部
Eulogizing the golden shower tree（detail）

玉樹臨風

The immortality and nobility of the Cypress

2016　紙本設色　74×45cm×4

中天明月懷蒼江

中天明月
Bright moon in the sky
2016　紙本設色　34×68.5cm

波瀾非信
Don't believe the ups and downs
2016 紙本設色 45×69cm

（左）唯證方知、（中）嚮於消長 、（右）清和當春

Only the enlightened can know, Toward growth and decline, Clear spring

2016　紙本設色　137×35cm×3

（左）無上況味、（中）陌上雲霓 、（右）遊遨及此

Supreme circumstances, Cloud and rainbow over the street, Roam here

2016　紙本設色　137×35cm×3

天邊玫瑰
Rose tinted horizon
2012　紙本設色　246×120cm

青鳥始信

The Beatitude of faith in a bluebird as
the harbinger of happiness.

2008　紙本設色　240×120cm

文化自覺

Cultural self awareness

1999　紙本設色　178×94cm

人文・自然

Culture and nature

1998　紙本設色　175×94cm

古風新象

New feel, old style

1999　紙本設色　178×95cm

天上人間

Heaven and earth

1999　紙本設色　177×95cm

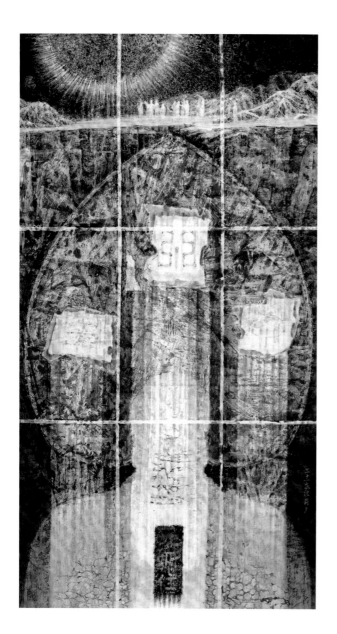

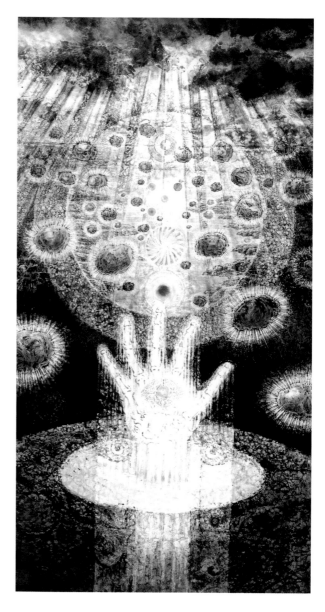

智的直覺

Instinct of wisdom

1999　紙本設色　177×96cm

文明省思

Civilized reflection

1999　紙本設色　178×96cm

若有所思

Thoughtful mind

2008　紙本設色　143×76cm

極春倚望

Rely on extreme goodness

2008　紙本設色　143×76cm

無意春聲

Inadvertent sounds of spring

2008　紙本設色　143×76cm

朝元

Chaoyuan

2008　紙本設色　68×47cm

揚清
Elimination
2016　紙本設色　45×35cm

上海梧桐
Shanghai phoenix tree
2012 紙本設色 143×76cm

東風西潮　Eastern style, Western fashion
1999　紙本設色　142×360cm

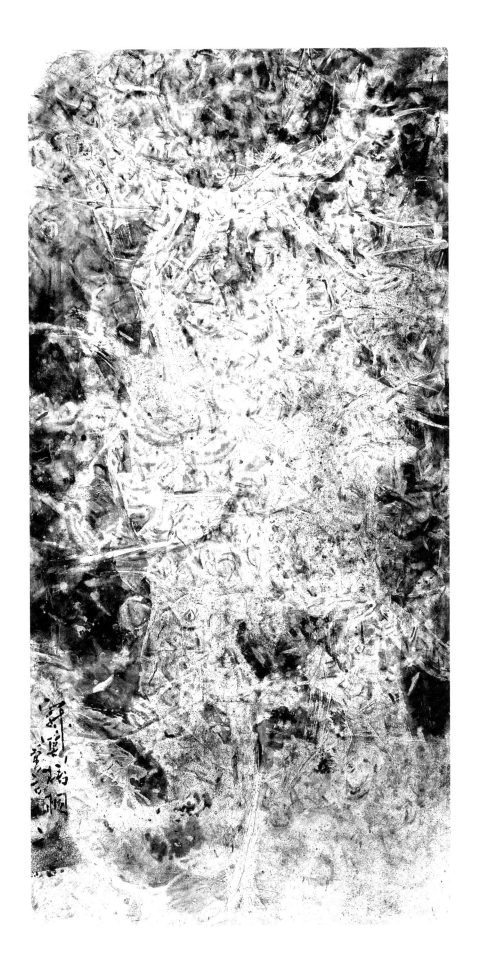

寂寞梧桐
Lonely phoenix tree
2012 紙本設色 143×76cm

含容空有

Inclusivity

2012　紙本設色　143×76cm

新月梧桐

New moon phoenix tree

2012　紙本設色　143×76cm

文心雕龍
The Literary Mind and the
Carving of Dragons
2012　紙本設色　143×76cm

曇花一現
Flash in the pan
2011　紙本設色　143×76cm

自在當初

At ease in the beginning

2016　紙本設色　69×45cm

仁愛之樹
Tree of Kindness and Love
2012 紙本設色 143×76cm

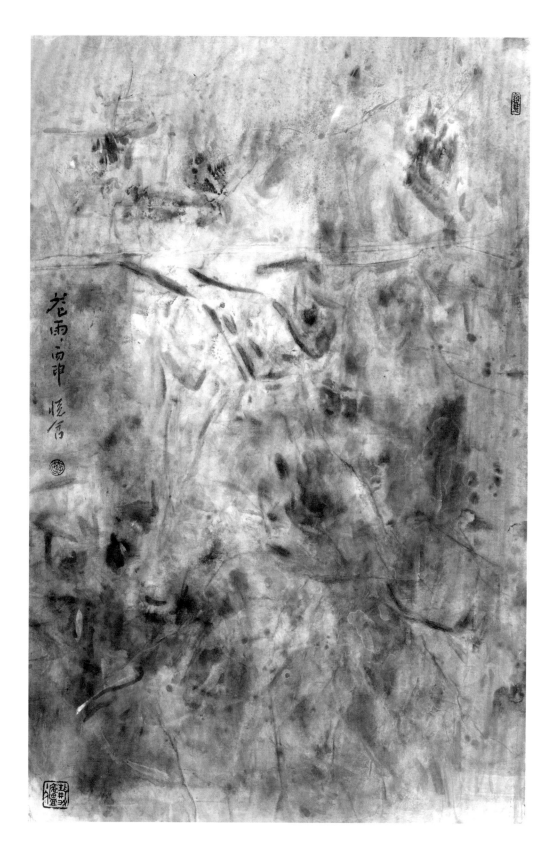

花雨
Flower shower
2016 紙本設色 69×45cm

問君何適

Ask the gentleman what is appropriate

2012 紙本設色 73×76cm

悟明藝象

Clear art epiphany

2012　紙本設色　97×60cm

觀空
Contemplating emptiness (detail)

觀空

Contemplating emptiness

2016　紙本設色　69×45cm

風動心門

The wind touches the heart

2012　紙本設色　97×60cm

夢迴東方
Dreams of returning
2013　紙本設色　137×68cm

荷月
Lotus moon
2008　紙本設色　45×67cm

靜影沉璧

Moon shadow on the water

2016　紙本設色　69×45cm

擬真

Simulation

2016　紙本設色　69×45cm

寂寞邊坡
Lonely slope
2012　紙本設色　143×76cm

月光寒吟

Reciting under the cold moon light

2008　紙本設色　76×70cm

誰能會心

Who can understand me?

2016　紙本設色　34.5×23cm

歡 · 101
Joy 101
2014　紙本設色　143×76cm

遠芳春意
Spring fragrance in the distance
2008　紙本設色　143×76cm

日上
Sunrise
2016 紙本設色 69×45cm

解夢花語 Dream interpretations and floral language
2002　紙本設色　59×96cm

生之禮讚　Tribute at birth
2002　紙本設色　59×96cm

向日朝陽

Worship the sun

2002　紙本設色　59.5×96.5cm

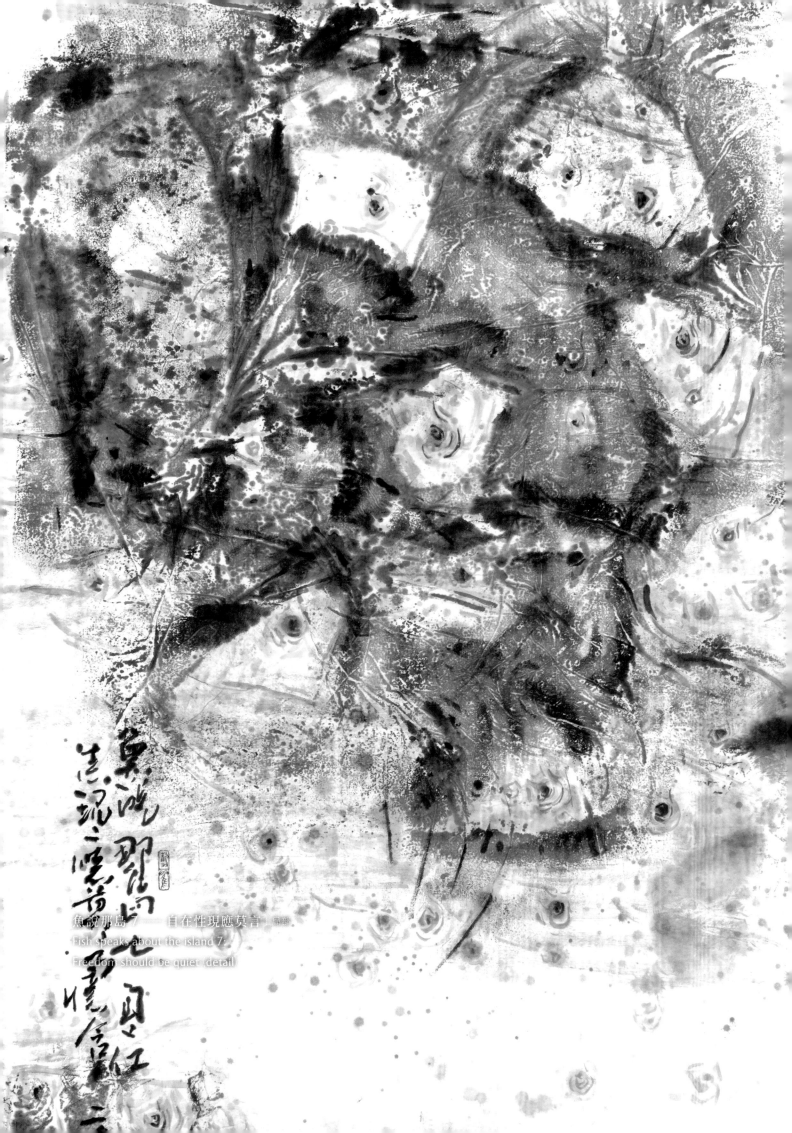

魚說那島 7——自在性現應莫言
Fish speaks about the island 7:
Freedom should be quiet detail

魚說那島 5 ── 水面風波我不知（局部）
Fish speaks about the island 5:
I know nothing of wind on the water (detail)

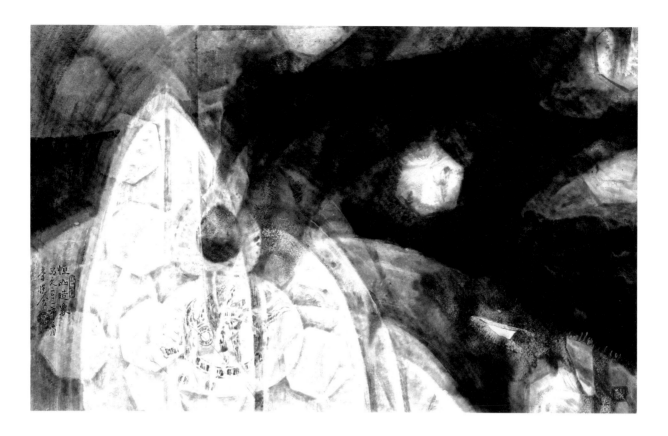

恆山造象　Hengshan image creation
2002　紙本設色　59×96cm

陽光聚會　Sunlight party
2002　紙本設色　60×96cm

光明在望

Hope in the light

2002　紙本設色　96×59cm

自性思維
Self-conscious thinking
2002　紙本設色　59×96cm

木蘭新象

New image of Mulan

1999　紙本設色　96×60cm

五嶽真形

The real Five Sacred Mountains

1999　紙本設色　95×58cm

星城記實

Star city record

1999　紙本設色　97.5×60cm

三月臺灣

Taiwan in March

1999　紙本設色　98×72cm

西藏之雲
Clouds of Tibet
2000 紙本設色 97.5×61cm

無華之華
Wonder in the unadorned
1999 紙本設色 90×57cm

造化之象　Image of Nature

1999　紙本設色　94×59cm

本立道生　The Way comes from the foundation
1999　紙本設色　90×62cm

Mother・臺灣
Mother Taiwan
2007　紙本設色　76×70cm

藍調夜曲
Rhythm and blues nocturne
2008　紙本設色　142×90cm

古道夢迴

Dreams of ancient paths

1998 紙本設色 93×62cm

自由心證

Free evaluation of evidence through inner conviction

1999 紙本設色 94×59cm

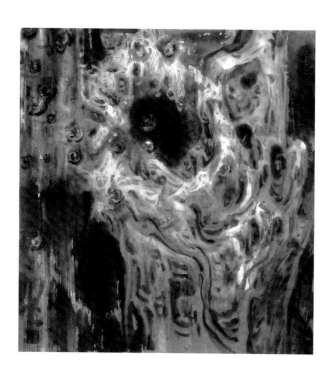

幸運石云

Lucky stone statement

2008 紙本設色 68×68cm

山東日照

Sunlight in Shandong

2004　紙本設色　60×97cm

蓮心自在
Freedom of the lotus heart
2008　紙本設色　68×68cm

顯見超情
Clear emotion
2012　紙本設色　70×68cm

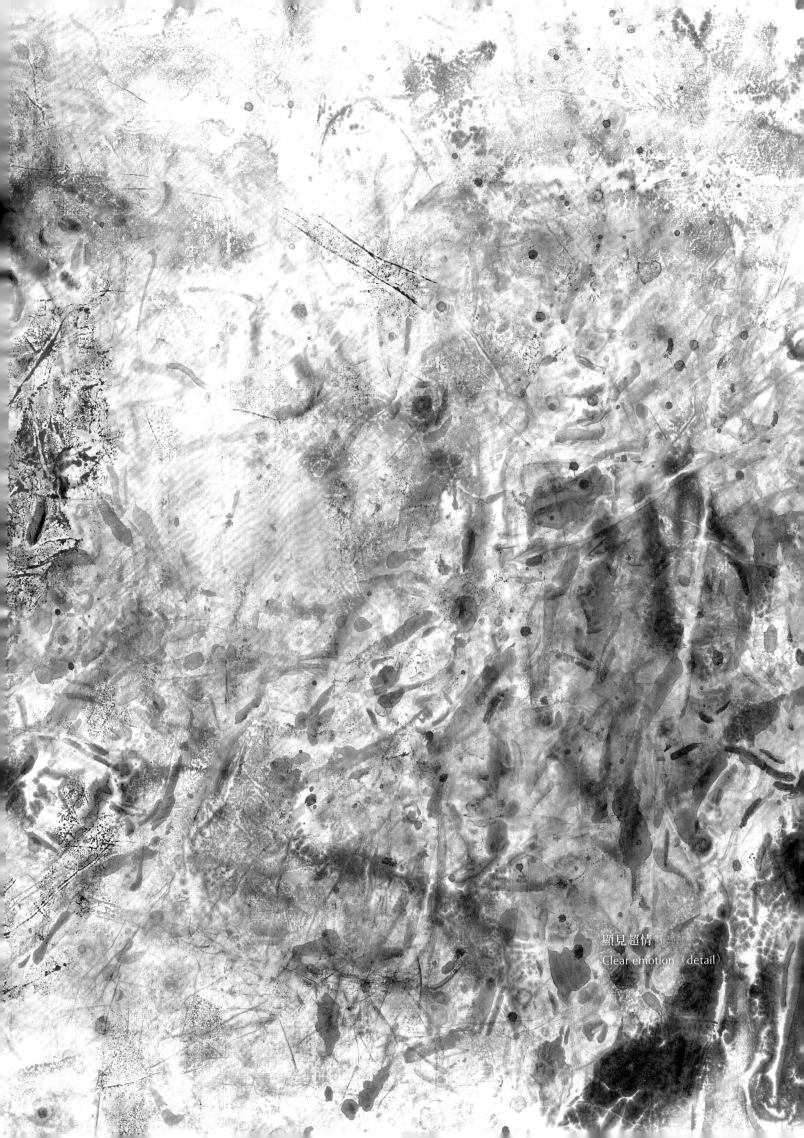

顯見超情（局部
Clear emotion（detail）

靈的動機
Spiritual motives
2012　紙本設色　69×68cm

藝道美學・靈動思惟

嗨！閻浮提
Hi! Yen Fu Ti

2012　紙本設色　69×68cm

顯見
Obvious
2016　紙本設色　69×45cm

八煙
Eight smokes
2016　紙本設色　34×45.5cm

中國風韻
Chinese China
1994　紙本設色　77×47cm

黃金海岸
Gold Coast
2002　紙本設色　45×68cm

春朝
Spring morn
2016 紙本設色 34×45.5cm

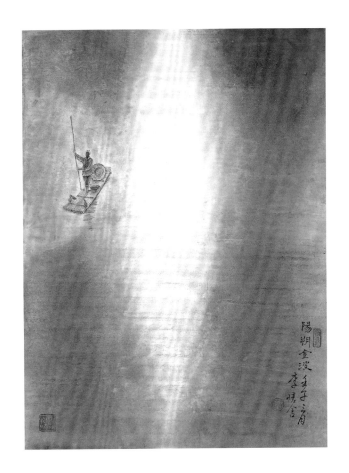

陽朔金波

Golden wave in Yangshuo

2002　紙本設色　45×34cm

燈火通明

A blaze of light

2000　紙本設色　45×34cm

雨中黃蟬 Yellow cicada in the rain

2002 紙本設色 45×68.5cm

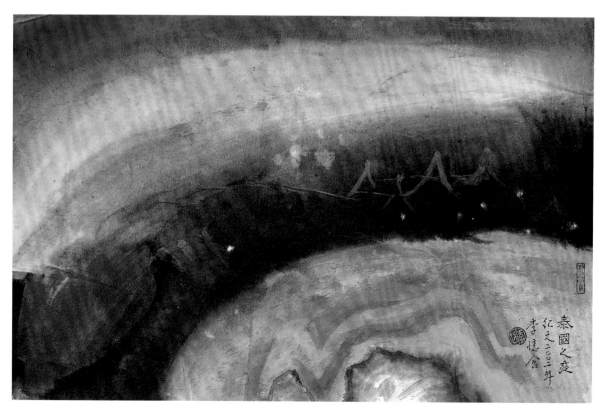

泰國之夜 Nighttime in Thailand

2002 紙本設色 41.5×65cm

山海經驗 Mountain and sea experiences

2004 紙本設色 46×69cm

西山龍門 Xishan Longmen

2004 紙本設色 46×69cm

古道幻象 Illusions of ancient ways

2004 紙本設色 46.5×68.5cm

喜出望外 Overjoyed

2004 紙本設色 46.5×68cm

顧盼

Look around

2016　紙本設色　69×45cm

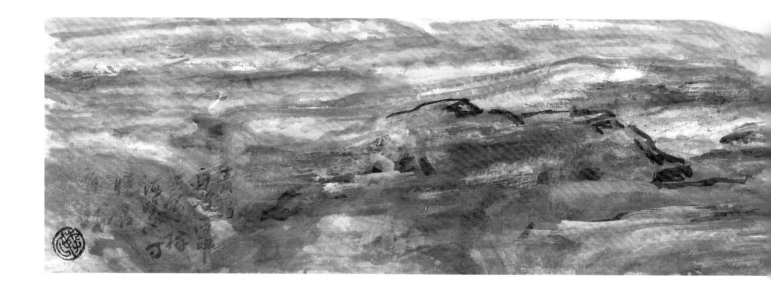

花東縱谷
Huadong Rift Valley
2016　紙本設色　9×69cm

青靄白波
Blue mist and white waves
2016　紙本設色　11×69cm

妙華

Miaohua

2008　紙本設色　68×47cm

興會

Flash of inspiration

2008　紙本設色　68×47cm

洛神
Roselle
2008　紙本設色　68×47cm

迷欲
Fascination
2008　紙本設色　68×47cm

論文——

體「時」用「中」的思考與實踐——李憶含

體「時」用「中」的思考與實踐

李憶含

壹、前言

當今在這文化全球化思潮之下，後現代情境所關注的當代性議題，仍存在許多不得不面對之歷史質問；以東方人文蘊涵來說，藉由精神性意義的積極重探，從中理解藝術文明之思想與觀念，並體會其所具有獨特審美意識之處，誠屬至關重要而且必要。因此，尋思透過主體心性的自然作用，映對傳統美學思想、呼應現代藝術觀念，以及顯明當代創作型態，除了使得風格圖式深刻而明徹之外，在生命境界上也能逐漸超越且昇華，進而領略其「含意奧妙」的理想所在。

有鑑於此，對於文化發展審度、歷史進程理解，乃至哲學理路詮釋的深入研究，理應明辨所謂「文化相對主義」（Culturalrelativism），既需清楚「文化精神」的再生意義，也要明白「藝術本質」之更新意識，此即為後現代理論的關鍵性思考。凡是具有主體自覺的當代學界人士，都應對理想之文化精神與藝術本質，有根本上的認知和省察。

因為，那不完全是東方與西方、傳統與現代、本土與國際、在地性與全球性的簡單思考，當然，也不應僅存妄想和偏執的文化臆測，抑或只是分別及對立之藝術忖度，而是體認其真實對應人性與文明，觸動兼具意識和精神的整體表現。

並且，源於一種歷史進程的意義審度，通過「主體精神性」（靈性）思惟，揭示兼具國際眼光與中心思想的見解；透過生活品質彰明文化精神，藉由創作內涵顯示藝術本質，使其象徵「靈感／興趣」之生命實踐，如實映照「究竟／真實」的智慧行止。

貳、全球化思潮下的藝道美學觀

基於此，有關本文之研究動機與目的，著實理應審視和重探：一、自主精神發展的階段性風格；二、超越意識型態的系統性圖式；三、東方超現實化的激觸與感發；四、當代唯易思想的辨析和證驗，期望以此感時契機、興中意會，揭示有機整體理論的融貫及建構。至於「藝道美學」之哲理觀解，既攸關「靈動思惟」的覺觀旨趣，也影響「精神高度」之悟明意向，其研究架構重點也就在於：通過靈動契機的「主體自覺」，呈現個人確認的「覺性明理」，映出親身實證之「悟道顯藝」，內容含涉主體精神性層面，可分為以下四點：1. 從探討人類演化的歷史進程中，明確存在意識與自我實現的審度；2. 從探討中西文化背景的差異中，釐正藝術根源與主體精神的契合；3. 從探討社會意識現象的觀察中，彰明現實與超現實的融合及運用；4. 從探討當代精神文明的生機中，揭顯東方特質與文化自覺的表現。

一、自主精神發展的階段性風格

昔日悠然的生命印象與美麗記憶，不但豐富了個人的自然經驗，也體現出自身之人文涵養，使得藝術契合主體的心靈意識。經由「精神性」理念的清楚確立，從中自己更加體認「藝術即道

理」，也就是説，既是一種正向、系統的風格發展，也是一種有機、整體之型態趨向，因此，有關人生種種的遷異與變化，包括生活、生存、生命之意識或覺察，除了説明時空更迭和境界轉換，無形中促進了藝術的「質／能」衍義，呈現出真實之「精／神」形象。

隨著時代、文化、社會的變化，探尋一種靈動、自然的生命狀態。或許是藝術觀念的選擇、堅持，呈顯的是近乎自由之情境、氛圍，亦是喻為自在的靈性、美感。期望如此擬人化之自然遷異，可以引發浪漫式的精神活動，演繹出自主、超越之藝術創造。在此，筆者就個人的生命實踐過程，説明有關自我追尋的主體狀態、精神理想的藝術境界，以及藝術探索的風格型態，並就藝術發展的階段性風格，除此繪畫啟蒙時期（1959 −）之外，予以簡明分為五個時期：

（一）傳統奠基時期（1969 −）

此一時期為繪畫初始的階段，在學習的內容上，以傳統水墨概念與西方繪畫知識為主，其中，學習過程是以循序漸進的方式，依照階段次第逐步地推展，以筆墨運用、傳摹臨寫，以及章法佈局之概念為主，從中隱約理解「筋骨血肉」的形質、表象，概略體會「意貫氣足」之神采、真實。

（二）自然探秘時期（1979 −）

此一時期為大學研究的階段，在學習的內容上，以「寫形狀物」、「探理覓趣」、「搜妙創真」為主，著重媒材技法與情景交融的研究，主要思想在於「外師造化」、「中得心源」與「通體皆靈」，期望藉由「造化之象」的客觀認知，理解「妙合天成」的主觀意趣，從中體會「生機勃發」之精神氣象。

（三）人文關懷時期（1997 −）

此一時期為碩士研究的階段，在學習的內容上，以「思想溯源」、「古風新貌」、「時代映象」為主，著重形式結構與創意造境之探討，主要藝術思想在於「含真藏古」、「培元固本」與「養正導和」，期望藉由「東方美學」的完整認知，理解「藝術創造」的真正意義，體會「文化自覺」之究竟理想。

（四）心靈究竟時期（2006 −）

此一時期為博士研究的階段，在學習的內容上，以「靈視意象」、「幻覺形態」、「潛意識流」為主，著重主題內容與觸機神應的探討，主要藝術思想在於「呼喚東方」、「水墨活著」與「靈動叫魂」，期望藉由「玄化秘境」的主觀認知，理解「精神覺照」的終極意旨，體會「靈動自然」之奧妙蘊涵。

（五）自有我在時期（2012 −）

雖説擬定此一「自有我在」時期，作為個人未來風格研究的階段，其實也是連結過去、延續現在，以及發展未來之研究主軸。這一階段以「變異現象」、「歸元本體」、「顯靈密趣」為主，著重終極意義與自我追尋的探討，主要思想在於「靈動天心」、「覺照人間」和「發明自己」，期望藉由「莊嚴理想」的概念認知，理解「極致現實」的心性意向，體會「清淨本然」之主體狀態。

由此觀之，自然真理並非固定化、不變化，或是意識化，而是超越美麗瞬間的生命究竟。同樣地，藝術信仰不是一種感性的妄想，不是一種理智的執著，而是一種理性的延伸。因此，無論是自然真理，抑或是藝術信仰，都是緣於生命自身而靈動起用，隨同主體心性而自然顯現，依循精神體會而道理明證。就藝術、宇

宙、人生的互通性而言，既是明證生存的意會、感通、靈覺，也是應驗生活的清淨、自在、解脫，更是體悟生命之自度合適。所謂「藝術／道理」即為：經由個人確認的「覺性明理」，親身實證之「悟道顯藝」，以期體現東方美學的「莊嚴性格」，證驗當代藝術之「通達義理」，由此一觀念延伸，我們可說主體心性的究竟顯明，既是主體精神的靈動功能，也是心性意識之自然作用。而且，精神自覺如同一種理智、感性、理性的度量衡，藝術理想猶似契機、明理、合道之超連結，這也似揭顯道理自在人心、藝術得於道理。

二、超越意識型態的系統性圖式

　　基於前述，筆者以源於主體人的靈動思惟，審視精神理想、重探生命本然，期望未來仍然依循「藝術／道理」，從本體、現象與作用層面的認識，探究水墨精神性之象徵意涵，而且，以客觀理性的方式，釐正東方美學內涵、精神與表現，審度當代藝術緣起、進行和狀態，積極尋求「盡性知天」的理想意義，以此作為「藝術自明」（evidente）之現實根據。

　　從碩士階段到博士研究的過程中，筆者基於回歸東方的思想理路，期望以此個人化的創作美學觀，明確審視靈的主體、重探活之精神，釐正藝學之道無他，但用此心而已。因此，採簡明扼要與概括統整的方式，將有關本文意向、領域、跨度，予以融會集成和貫通理路，使其盡量符合內容的論述需要。如同中庸章句所謂心法傳授，「其書始言一理；中散為萬事；末復合為一理。放之，則彌六合；卷之，則退藏於密。」然而，有鑑於當代藝術思潮的多元化發展，相關的美學思想與藝術理論，呈現出既複雜且繁殊之演繹趨向。由於學養權衡與識見考量，期冀論述形式有所規範和限制，以免內容呈顯欠缺明確旨趣或意向。換言之，本論文只是此一階段歷程中，就有關美術研究和創作理論層面，作概括式經驗綜合與心得整理，並將研學治藝所面臨的問題和困難，予以系統性的梳理及探勘。同時，希望從中明確主體心性的自然作用，理解東方美學之精神蘊涵，以及體會當代藝術的實質意義，並將此作為日後在思考與實踐，以期形塑融會的藝術觀念和風格表現，其中有關東方超現實畫風、靈視‧幻象演繹，乃至觸機神應的印證，則是在於明證超越意識型態的系統性圖式。（表1）

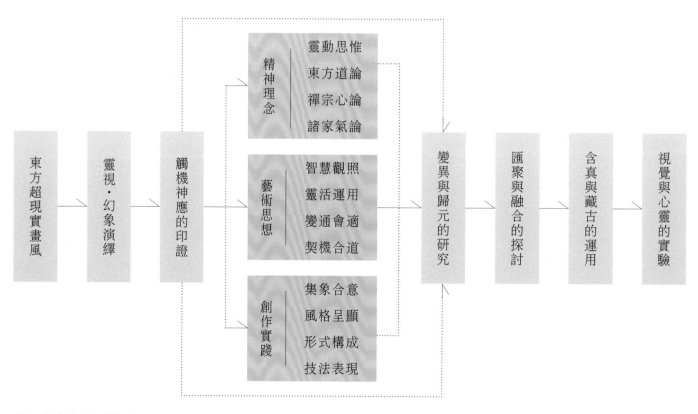

表1：論文書寫架構說明

三、東方超現實化的激觸與感發

一般而言，多元化現象說明自然法則與自由意志。同時，也寓意某種人性和文明之間的對應關係，揭示了客觀世界的「隨機」應變，以及主觀世界之「自由」互動，這種「預先」與「決定」的構成規律，確實是一種極其特殊的演繹型態，也是一種不可臆測之經驗意涵。透過直覺感通所體會到自由意志，正是其具有生命意向的明白覺察。在藝術創作的積極審度上，表達具有思想與感情的美感意象，呈現出隨機和自由之風格型態，顯然需要秉持「安身立命」的精神理想，以「靈動契機」的美學思想，依「自然合道」之藝術觀念，呈現出「靈覺本真」的創作風格，真實體會《孟子‧盡心上》所言：「盡其心者，知其性也，知其性則知天矣。[1]」筆者嘗試以靈動思惟的自主與超越，結合古已有之的觸機和神應，作為東方超現實的藝術演繹觀，以此明證東西方哲學之思想融會，進而依智慧觀照的良知與妙顯，對應精神自覺之主體和心理，演成當代意義性的創作思想論。並且，將有關傳統、現代、當代的藝術型態，予以系統地精神貫通、整合聯繫，以此「靈視、幻象」與潛意識流，探討彩墨超現實畫風的符號、象徵與意涵。使得集象合意的「美」、「妙」之中，呈現出理想的風格呈顯、形式構成，以及技法表現。在此，筆者以「觸機神應」的延伸思考，概述個人創作實踐之理論依據：

（一）觸機神應與變通會適的認知

由《周易‧繫辭傳下》「唯變所適」的理解，可知盡心知性能夠彰明客觀世界影響，自是產生迥然不同的心理反應。這種蘊藉奇妙的心理反應，改變了創作者自己的精神意向，也決定了主體對於現實世界的觀點，如同韓康伯注云：「變通貴於適時，趣舍存乎其會。」[2]因此，作為一個主體自覺的藝術家，一個高度思想的創作者，既須清楚「自我本性」與「自然道體」，也要明白「生命精神」和「藝術本質」，源於觸機神應與變通會適的認知，透過精神覺照以「洞性靈之奧區」，從中理解「靈」活「運」用的經驗過程，體會精神理想之象徵與意義。同時，覺察「唯變所適」的思想和觀念，揭顯藝術創造之觀照及思惟；清楚所謂的「精神／自然」，就在於主體的「靈覺／感通」，明白所謂的「藝術／靈動」，就在於自覺的「唯易／思想」。

（二）觸機神應與美感意象的覺察

美感除了需要具備主觀審美經驗之外，也需要客觀美學規則的條件。美確實不可能憑空想像，它必須依附於具體物象之上，緣此，藝術之美成為現世生活、精神理想，甚或主體意涵上的折衷與融合，換言之，即為一種觸機和神應的美感意象。創作者依據自身的歷史、文化與民族等背景，對於有關時代、地域、事件的意識或覺察，與其感官經驗及視覺記憶整合，表達理性、感性和理智之內在體驗，呈現出內心世界的精神狀態。因此，透過觸機神應與美感意象的相互映照，使得藝術意義的對應詮釋、覺性解讀，能夠為鑑賞者意會或感知其旨趣所在，理解其所代表時代意義和文化自覺，從作品的形式及內容來看，也可探悉創作者對於藝術本質的精神體會，此等喻為獨自的內在靈視，誠屬一種自我本性的關懷（thought of the self）。

（三）觸機神應與興會意義的體會

從當代（現代）與當代藝術的探究中，可知由於感官的意識作用和外界相互連繫，在經由不斷延展、重疊及再生的過程中，逐漸形成種種的觀念演繹，擴大認知上的範圍與層面。因此，藉由東西美學思想與哲學理論的研究，理解文化意識中有關感性的直覺（intuition），與理智、理性之間的相互作用。同時，明白東西雙方對於事物的探究，中國傾向於感性直覺與精神體悟，是以心靈覺照的方式體驗真實；西方則著重在客觀理

1　史次耘註譯，《孟子今註今譯》（臺北：臺灣商務，2009），375。
2　（魏）王弼著、（晉）韓康伯著，《周易王韓注》（臺北：大安出版，1999），229。

智和科學分析，是以心理感知的方式探究表徵。透過相關資料彙集與梳理，更加體會心的狀態和精神作用，從中清楚感性直覺、明白精神體悟，除了確認主體能動的心性意向，對美的本質之感觀與感受，也有深刻映對的覺察和悟出。基於「本立道生」的心領神會，尋思經由審美活動與藝術創造，演成「會相歸體」之經驗總結，進而釐清東西方藝術的風格和範疇，概述當代藝術之多元化演繹，顯示其中各異其趣的表現特質。（表2）

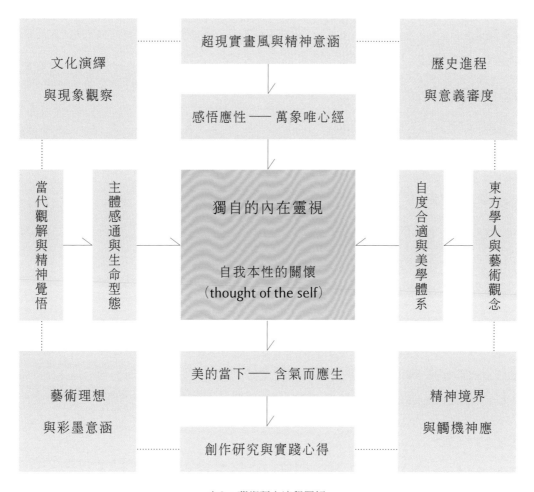

表2：藝術研究流程圖解

四、當代唯易思想的辨析和證驗

　　有關本文研究的方法與範圍，是以研學治藝的經驗體證為主，內容包括精神理念、藝術思想，以及創作實踐層面，並就美術理論與創作研究的心得，依學術研究的方式予以整理記錄，使用研究方法包括理論研究法、比較研究法與實驗研究法。為避免因模糊或空洞的浮泛言說，使得內容繁衍而顯得不夠嚴謹，在研究方法與方向上，也因個人能力未及而有所限制，在此僅依據現階段研究、探索與實驗的歷程，將歷程中所認知、理解和體會的相關資訊、知識、理論，予以結體彙集與系統整合。至於研究過程所面臨的問題與困難，選擇以概括性的析出方式，將其歸納、統合，或略作梳理與探勘。可見理解「自度合適」的藝術表現，即為清楚研究原則與明白研究限制，而靈動思惟之藝術表現，既在明確藝術是知識性或智覺性，也在釐正美術是物質化或精神化，同時，更在審度水墨是科學型或哲理型，以此作為個人式藝術解決方案，誠屬一種當下性的思考與抉擇。茲依序分述如下：

（一）精神理念層面

　　以藝術形式與內容而言，通常和當今美學思想、藝術理論及創作表現有關。因此，在研究方向的探討上，顯然是需要具有系統結構與有機整合，除此，也需要注重心靈與意識的互通聯繫，強調理論和風格之觀念創新，更要兼具思考及實踐的發展可能。以此緣故，筆者擬定自然、人文與心靈的探索取向，作為重要的參考資料，並且，就「靈視、幻象與潛意識流」的角度，深刻地探索當代藝術諸多問題，以及其背後蘊含的文化動因，進而透過相關思想與理論的研究，使得藝術具有「古今精神承傳」、「中西思想匯通」的特性，同時，也期望作品之中顯示文化自覺的理念，呈現符應東方精神的水墨美學意涵。

（二）藝術思想層面

　　二十一世紀當代藝術思潮的多元化傾向，呈現出急遽的變遷與轉型，顯示出複雜繁殊的藝術發展。有關超現實繪畫風格的概念指涉，一般多數認為屬於西方藝術的風格型態，然而，其中有關知識性與智覺性、物質化與精神化，以及科學型與哲理型等等，仍然有待進一步分辨或釐清。不可否認地，藝術是源自人類的心靈活動，是精神性表現的「自然形象」，也是東方中國原始社會的共通內容，可見超現實繪畫風格的表現形式，其實早已存在於古代中國。當今文明危機與衝突日益嚴重，顯示出人們對心的作用之誤解，由於過度衍異的意識操作，導致主體的情感凝滯與精神困乏。作為人類心靈導向的藝術思潮，是否能夠真正喚起生命的覺醒，成為一種「明心見性」的精神救贖，應是諸多有心人士的共同期望。

（三）創作實踐層面

　　藝術創作實是在自我「明心」之中，尋求自然「見性」的心靈活動，因此，如何在動機、方向、目的中，明確適合自己之研學方法，經由按部就班地理解、依次漸進地深入探究，並且，採取階段性目標、逐步地加以完成。基於此，擬想透過美術理論與創作研究，使得源於「靈動契機」、「詩興明理」，以及「自然合道」，呈顯「道存／靈活」、「藝在／運用」；首先，確立在精神理念上的自我定位或定向；其次，呈現出有關理論的概念、觀念與意念的整體構思；再者，經由藝術思想的系統架設，自然落實於創作實踐中；最終，盼望以完整而全面性的觀解，真實體證藝術的意義與價值，使得個人化的藝術觀點、見解和主張，在東西藝術思想的理論體系上，能有具體而明確的方式作為遵循及依據。

　　綜合前述，可見當代唯易思想的辨析與證驗，是在「美藝／融會」和「靈智／貫通」的探究上，思考經由「東西遇合」的精神體會，回歸生命本身之「感覺／統合」。換言之，期盼通過「凝神專注」的研學治藝，顯明「變通會適」之創作實踐，這樣一來，即可映照出如同宗白華所言，具有宇宙美、人生美與藝術美，此外，尋求相應於心靈本質的視覺語言，形塑象徵意識型態、情感場面，以及哲理架構之觀念系統。選擇適切的圖式風格與象徵符號，透過智性思惟之建構方式，表達蘊含自然、真實的創作旨趣，進而以濃厚的詩意美感，詮釋含義奧妙而獨特之靈視場域。以靈動意趣契應真實智慧的體證，揭示「物理—生理—心理—命理—道理」的關係，呈現具有東方精神的美感意象，傳達隱含當代意識之自我感受。同時，顯示一種周旋、迴盪般的藝術風水觀，即為探求靈性導啟的精神性思惟，企盼臻於智慧彰顯之自然能量場。（表3）

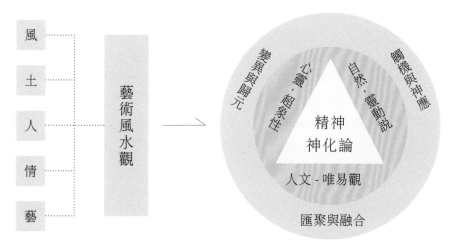

表3：氣化流行與藝術風水觀示意圖

參、有機整體理論的融貫及建構

　　在本文研究的階段過程中，主要依據美術理論與創作研究的實踐，透過東西方美學思想和藝術理論的運用，從中體會藝術的當代功能與積極意義。筆者認為經由持之以恆的研究與探討，除了可提供現階段創作方向的思考，也能彙集相關理論研究的參考資料。因此，在自我追尋與藝術探索中，極力探求符應超現實性的風格面向，期望能夠契合於自己的生命實踐。再者，藉由此一文本脈絡的整體審視，試圖建構一種蘊含精神理念、藝術思想，以及創作實踐的有機系統理論，使其成為學術研究與資源整合的參考。

　　藝術創作過程是經由題材內容的選擇、形式結構的探討、材質媒介的的運用，以及表現技法的研發，而予以具體化的整全呈現。其中經由觀察、想像、體驗的方式，隨其性質內涵、象徵意義，在感性與理性交替作用之下，經由選擇、組合、表現的過程，將作者情感、思想與創意理念靈動落實，使作品形式、本質和內容意涵自然轉化，成為具有獨特意義的藝術作品。有感於現代（當代）藝術的多元面向、雜沓紛陳，擬以蘊含文化自覺的思想、自由表現的理路，積極探討各種風格、形式與技法，並在內涵視覺化的演變過程，反覆研究造型、色彩、肌理等繪畫元素，期望以最好的構成和適切的風格，表現出作品本身的精神意涵。因此，以「靈視、幻象與潛意識流」為主要的研究內容，並採取下列三種探索方向，探討「彩墨超現實畫風的符號、象徵與意涵」。並就其可能發展的風格和樣式，乃至預期目標及成果，經由簡明構思與概括言說，分別予以條列如下：

（一）傳統研究與突破

　　有關傳統研究與突破的創作思考，主要是以文化精神和獨特風格為取向。探研傳統美學精華而予以現代轉化，並且，融會各種民族的文化特質，積極拓展具有藝術理想之風格型態。使其形成多元互生的精神實體，彰明具有傳統質素、靈活思想與創意表現，進而形塑蘊含東方特色的語言系統。在明白研究旨意或創作趣向，期許自己能夠「一以貫之」，而且持之以「正」（恆常），羅之以「芳」（詩興），竭誠以「盡心知性」，由「知性」發明「自己」，而後秉志虔誠、「守之不動」，能夠因之以「知天」（悟道）。

（二）現代探索與創新

　　有關現代探索與創新的創作思考，主要是以時代特性和藝術精神為取向，探究創意造型及風格圖式的觀

念，呈現具有情思美感的特質。因此，筆者將「藝術」視為「道體」，一種隱含精神承載之理想「實體」，亦即如同生命型態般的有機整體。這種「實體」猶似身、心、靈的異質同構，其演繹或衍異的種種過程與現象，儼如是物質和精神之間的自然轉化，也是一種變異及歸元的「靈動現象」。期冀以現代視野表現新題材與內容，呈現新形式和技法的視覺效果，使畫作具有獨特的藝術特質及精神面貌。

（三）前衛實驗與發展

有關前衛實驗與發展的創作思考，主要是以心靈意識和實驗探索為取向，掌握當代藝術思潮的精神內涵，重新建構審美理想及價值意義，感應當下現實的情境氛圍，揭發蘊含精神氣動之內在真實，以偶然性的趣味、多元性的手法，甚至破壞性的觀念表現。在理解藝術的變異與歸元中，探尋契合自我的精神理想和藝術境界。對於傳統、現代、當代的藝術型態，嘗試以「生命永續」與「精神常存」的體會，依「觸機神應」和「良知妙顯」之感通，採「東方前衛」及「當代逸境」的覺察，探討彩墨超現實畫風的符號、象徵與意涵。

簡而言之，此一有機整體理論的融貫及建構，是以理論研究法、比較研究法與實驗研究法，依藝術理念的研究、創作表現的探索和風格型態的實驗，目的在於呈現傳統研究與突破、現代探究與創新，乃至前衛實驗與發展，期望風格建構映對主體心性，自然顯明東方理想的藝術之道，同時，也是對精神理解與藝術詮釋的審視，對文化背景和心理結構之重探。因此，無論是「藝術→道理」、或是「道理←藝術」，主要在於揭顯「道存／靈活」、「藝在／運用」，如實映對心中理想的形象投射，藉此明確精神自覺與文化特質，釐正美學思想和藝術理論。也就是說，除了將精神理念與美學旨趣的關鍵論述，做一種簡明且概括的融貫統攝，並把個人研究內容與主要觀點，依序予以整全的梳理和條列，以期釐清東方精神的「自主／功能」、當代意義的「超越／作用」，甚或主體心性的「藝術／理想」，藉以完整闡發靈動思惟之「象徵／意涵」，換言之，即透過「歸元本體」、「變異現象」的相互對應，呈現中得心源之「顯靈密趣」，以此延伸美術理論與創作實踐。（表4）

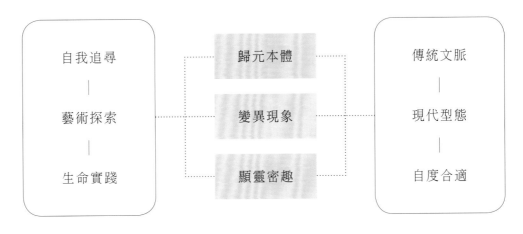

表4：超現實畫風與顯靈密趣示意圖

一、「靈動‧契機」的變通會適

藝術造形（Art Formation）屬於一種視覺創造，是運用視覺創造力的表現模式，創作者將藝術所涵具的情思美感，轉換成具體可視（及可觸）之形象特徵，並將其自然整合、真實傳達給觀賞者，使其具有同樣情思美感之創造過程。視覺傳達源起於藝術造形的表現，融會於整個藝術表現領域之內，因此，探討映照主體心性的視覺創造，自是應由美感理論與藝術構成中，予以系統性的研究和探討。

一般而言，藝術家通常側重於形象思維，是以凝神專注方式觀看世界，其特點是思維形象直觀、觀察精確敏銳。在客觀的現實生活之中，發現富有盎然生機與情思意趣，進而將美感特質創造出藝術意象。通過主觀意識將無形的思維，轉化為有形的思維，使得整體活動更具清晰性和條理性。如德國哲學家康德（Immanuel Kant, 1724-1804）所言：只從事於認識之想像力範疇，是在悟性約束之下受到限制，以期切合這種悟性的概念。但在審美企圖、想像活動是自由的，以在其對概念協合一致外，對悟性未被搜尋、內容豐富的，及未曾開展過的悟性，在其概念裡未顧到的資料。在這場合裡悟性運用此等資料，不僅為使客觀地達到明確認識，而是主觀地自然生動以認識諸力，因此間接地也用於觀念認識。[3]

由此可見，藝術活動之觀念寓意的重要性，攸關「靈動‧契機」的變通會適，換言之，即在作品中呈現主體之情理蘊涵，透過靈活運用的綜合思維，將可達到觀念認識之「觸類旁通」，而激發個人的靈感與創意。在創作中以客觀現實的「物」，作為主觀引發靈感源泉之「因」，不斷的經由研究、探索與試驗，極力以求突破常規的制約和影響；創作者以「盡心知性」的靈覺理路，依自由構想之感通取徑，體會「以心印心」的藝術創造，即為精神與物質之連結關係。從這個意義上講，「悟道顯藝」的象徵意涵，如同在想像（神思）之形成階段，主體賦予客觀物象各種比擬。通過審美觀念演進、持續轉化自然，使得創意形象恰如其分，讓那造型寓意自然生動，逐漸符合自己的審美理想。如此一來，這種擬化的「悟道／形象」，也就成為靈化之「顯藝／對象」，此一妙不可言的契「機」合「道」，顯示「靈」活「運」用，確實與主體之人的心理有關。

二、「詩興‧明理」的本質還原

其實藝術創作活動的具體實踐，可說是一種精神理念的物質化過程，也是藝術形式為內容服務的現實性觀點。再者，藝術形式能夠呈現主體精神意向，反映人自身的獨特個性，是表達情思美感和主體精神之載體。一般而言，為形式而形式或為內容而內容的觀念，也許有其某種審美趣味或價值功用，但若是過度偏向為形式或為內容之「執著」，對真正的藝術創作顯然都是不切實際。況且，在藝術創作的表現過程中，將形式與內容予以勉強分離，將會造成形式圖解內容，或者內容約束形式之問題呈現。因此，理解藝術內容與形式的相互關係，是隨著人（主體）與自然（客體）之有機聯繫，而呈現出內在真實的心靈感應，同時，這種蘊藏生命動能的「潛意識」，有其極為特殊的連結方式，著實是因人而異、隨時轉移，而且是應運而生、隨機變換。基於此，嘗試以內容與形式的契合關係，研究現代藝術中「觸機神應」的精神理念；並從本質上，探討東西方的文化精神與藝術特徵。筆者認為，東方超現實畫風的理解與詮釋，其中主要的美學思想，實是源於主體精神的「靈動思惟」，而基本的藝術觀念，則是緣起心性意識的「智性思惟」，期望透過主體心性的自然作用，映對哲學思辨與精神覺照，呈現出靈活生動的風格型態，如此一來，既可闡明「體—相—用」的藝術真如觀，又能呈顯「身—心—靈」之整體性思維，使其成為理想藝術的特殊言境，具體傳達「真—善—美」的精神化蘊涵。（表5）

表5：哲學思辨與精神覺照示意圖

3　宗白華、韋卓民等譯，《判斷力批判》（臺北：滄浪出版，1986），168。

在當代藝術急遽演變的過程中，關於藝術思想與表現形式的探討，誠屬至關重要。我等身為藝術的創作者，自是應當明確所謂「藝術意義」，並且，尋思以「尊重己靈」的精神理想，審度主體本身的自覺性，關注藝術理想的精神性。也就是說，經由高度的哲思內省，對自己內在的心靈狀態有所覺知，通過專注的凝神觀照，從中體證個人與生俱來的生命真實。同時，基於人的根源性，重探主體心性的自然作用，釐正藝術創作的意義所在。如此一來，即可確立「藝術自明」的真正旨趣，實是精神自然、藝術靈動，進而透過哲學思想的觀念啟發，以期理解東方精神、詮釋當代意義，體會何為道理清楚、事實明白。基於這個觀念，在主觀解讀藝術創作過程中，應當可確認「詩興‧明理」的本質還原，映對自然、人文與心靈的互通性關係。在此，筆者就個人主要的九次展覽，依序說明有關藝術的思考與實踐，期望經過觀察、想像、體會，顯示出藝術理想之「靈的興會」；進而藉由選擇、組合、表現，呈現出精神境界之「美的創造」。將彼之感受、審思—內之在「意」，讓此之覺察、顯明—外之在「象」，使其成為具有精神意境的藝術現象。茲概略分列如下：

（一）「亙古的太魯」系列期（1984 －）

「亙古的太魯」之系列創作，純粹由傳統美學的語言表現，試圖營造文人化之山水意境，傳達出一種精神性的創作旨趣，顯明象徵「天人合一」之思想境界。此一系列不僅是自然景象的擬態與研究，也是個人對於精神氣度之觀象和探討，這種經驗歷程在藝術格局的開展，確實有著極為深遠之影響，譬如說，八〇年代以後的巨幅創作形式，顯然受到這一時期的激發與影響。「亙古的太魯」系列的創作，是以花蓮太魯閣一帶景象為主題，太魯景象屬於開放性展示系統，其中主要景觀有峻秀峽谷、清澈溪水、美麗雲海，以及岩石褶皺和蓊鬱森林，可謂兼具自然生態與人文景觀之美。

（二）「月世界幻象」系列期（1988 －）

「月世界幻象」之系列創作，主要是以藉景抒情的表現方式，透過自然景象之寓意顯明己見，因此，不僅在於客觀現實的形式探討，也是一種個人精神寫照之內容表達。長久以來，月世界的印象總是縈迴心懷，一九八八年專程前往迷幻異域、期盼一探究竟，綜觀無垠淒然景象，眼前呈現——果真如此，那般灰白泥山、孤立長亭、荒疏枯棘，環顧四周幾乎空無一人，儼然蔚為臺灣島嶼另一奇觀。日後每當筆者憶起彼時所見，依然有感於斯景蕭索、形同荒漠，那時心中隱含幾許悲愴觸發，似乎有一種難以言喻之情。或許，這般真實對應激越一種莫名悸動，既是主體心境與外境的靈動相應，也是當下景情遇合的自然感通。

（三）「臺灣－印象」系列期（1992 －）

昔時傳統化的臺灣，對中華古代文化思想的關注，民族認同情感的連結，甚或歷史記憶故事的延續，總是令人精神牽繫、無法忘懷。如果說浩瀚的太平洋，映襯著美麗的臺灣風光，那麼，這般奇偉的大自然，將是烘托出獨特的寶島名勝。臺灣懷古的風土人情、璀璨的人文光華使我沉醉，這是臺灣給人柔和、包容的印象；今日現代化的臺灣，記錄著四百年的歷史文化，卻始終以深情眷顧著藝術精華，其宏觀視野拓展生民未有的願景，如同今日臺北「101」的精神氣度，標示一種文明發展的時代象徵，彷彿以高聳入雲、傲然雄視之姿，環顧著當代社會的繁衍狀態，希冀以剛毅、堅韌的真實本質，依積極、肯定的超然屬性，運用象徵光明精神的東方智慧，持續導引臺灣自覺的靈動演藝。

（四）「東方／新象」系列期（1996 ─）

關於「千禧年」之藝術省思，個人的心理確實深感悲嘆與欣悅，而「後現代」情境引發心理焦躁和徨惑，更是令我無以自期、百感交集。因此，筆者以「古今精神承傳，中西思想匯通」，做為此一時期主要的探索面向，同時，以契合於東方精神的藝術風格、形式、技法，表達自己對於多元文化的哲理思辨，期望藉由精神互通性的理想，跨開東方水墨與西方繪畫之間的藩籬。也就是說，不把水墨性格侷限於物質性思維，而是以明確的精神性覺照，在具有高度文化理念中，將中國傳統水墨精華萃取、凝聚，並且經由完整的審視、重探，朝向現代（當代）藝術的轉變、化成，明證古今本相續的理想旨趣，應驗中外何需分之現實義理。

（五）「萬象唯心經」系列期（2000 ─）

此一宗教與藝術結合的積極嘗試，具有哲學和與靈智之象徵性寓意。意即個人亟欲以精神體會，透過覺觀與藝道的密切關係，映照心靈和意識之間互通性。在圖像符號的表現上，是以寓意沉默以對的自主性，表達出自我內省的存在感，從中透露一種寧謐自處之理想意趣，因此，「靈覺／感通」在作品中依舊是重要質素。就整體風格內容而言，似乎逐漸傾向於心靈的究竟，筆者刻意營造出晶瑩剔透的畫面效果，展現有如形變、質化之創意造型，使得作品略帶有冥想風似的靈性思索，表現一種儼如神秘主義之玄妙意味。這種趨於超現實畫風的過渡、轉變，主要是源於內在層面之覺觀、悟明。

（六）「繁華緣夢生」系列期（2002 ─）

從某種角度而言，此系列或可說是一種藝術變相，也是個人創作歷程的轉捩點，因這時期在思想內容與精神蘊涵，不但更明顯具有理想化藝術傾向，也蘊含一種超現實的風格特質。在藝術探索的實踐面向，確實不同於以往強調形式、技巧。由於水墨是東方特殊的媒材屬性，擬想以此材質的傳統經驗來延伸，但不像之前系列風格型態，極為講究構圖上的統合、完整。從此一時期的形式與內容中，可見往常的慣性思維已逐漸消解，這一系列雖然少了往日的穩定、執著，卻多了一些主觀的想像、表現。此時的水墨以「融貫中西」的方式呈現，甚至於將創意思考積極延伸，擴展到多媒材界面上的探索。

（七）「擬化現代荷」系列期（2004 ─）

二〇〇四年之後的系列作品，除了意味著主觀的情境表現之外，創作方式也由「法」（法執）而「化」（法化），儼如形變質化、舉重若輕一般，是把技巧藏於無形之中。此一看似輕而易舉的形象特徵，在於簡化實體的靈驗造型，不在於追求精湛之意趣表現，而是讓人聯想到一種非常「自然」。這般幻化似的符號與意象的轉型，即為視覺效果朝心靈意蘊之轉向，如此喻意隱藏式的表現型態，間接說明個人內在之激越、動盪。這種心靈動向的轉變與表現，有別於以往之拘理性、嚴謹，顯然比起過去更為自由、開放，而在於思想層面上，也更加趨向多元而靈活，平添許多奇譎、幻化的不確定性，或許可說是一種另類禪定之自在性。

（八）「靈視‧幻象」系列期（2008 ─）

此一系列包括「靈視‧幻象」之產生、運用、體會，以及其與藝術創作的關係。擬定以靈視意象、幻覺形態、潛意識流，探究「真實」建構與「虛擬」判別，依此演繹成超現實的玄化秘境，顯示為一種藝術本質之再思考。並且，從傳統、古典的繪畫研究中，理解何謂「美學能靜」；在現代、浪漫的創作表現裡，明白何為「藝術會動」。同時，審視傳統、古典與現代、浪漫之間，存在一種永恆精神的互通性，進而對東方水

墨、西方藝術的內在實質，加以全面而整體之明澈理解。期望在當代意義的層面上，經由高度思想的精神體會，尋求彼此相應之靈魂契合點，揭示符契「擬道化」的摩天氣象，呈顯近乎「靈覺化」之基本見解。

其中有關靈動思惟的美學向度，除了「詩興‧明理」的本質還原，主要基於東方道論的理序義、禪宗心論的生生義，以及諸家氣論的變化義，即為依審視主觀心知的執取面相，以重探藝術覺觀之真正意謂。並且，從道理真實的自然理則之中，關注當代思想的語言異化，換言之，就藝術本體、現象與作用上，釐定諸多衍義及其關聯特性，避免心知和語言的不當運作。因此，尋思經由傳統脈絡、現代型態的觀念理解，明確符應生命實踐之自我追尋，同時，釐正個人精神意向的藝術探索，以期詮釋「靈動生意」之風格象徵。此一思想理路意即在於：使得「美學能靜」的東方思想，彰顯主體精神之靈動功能；讓那「藝術會動」之當代企圖，導啟心性意識的自然作用，呈顯具有哲學高度、情感廣度，以及精神深度。概括而言，以藝術「體知」的思維方式，既在於闡明新人文的精神意涵，也在於揭示新文人之情感形式。就靈動思惟的藝術探索來講，歷來先哲前賢的真知灼見，蘊含自然、人文與心靈之精神企盼，呈顯寓意時代、民族和社會之文化展望，映現主體意會、感通及靈覺的象徵內容。由於具有淑世關懷的精神理念，不但顯示出對於生命本身的重視，也呈現出對於文化自主、藝術自由，乃至主體自覺的關注，此等明達人類精神文明的奧秘，堪稱契合全方位文化人之遠見。

（九）從「文心雕龍‧十式」──談當代水墨的視覺語言與特質（2017 -）

自從接觸正統繪畫訓練以來，迄今研學治藝近四十年，除了致力於藝術的教學與研究，並定期發表學術性論文和評述。2012年世界末日那天，筆者榮獲臺灣師範大學藝術學博士，其間，深刻理解東方理想的藝術之道，在於主體心性的自然作用，即以意識毀滅與靈智新生，因而更進一步地積極探索，期望經由覺觀主體、悟明心性，揭示文化意涵、藝術旨趣。之後，在臺北國立國父紀念館，舉辦了「東方‧凝視」-2017李憶含書畫藝術創作跨年特展。從展覽主題與作品名稱，似乎可看出其中端倪，此一基於絕對精神、積極意識，即為所謂「靈」活「運」用；換言之，源於東方獨特的藝道精神，既屬震旦氣象的生命原型，也是華夏文明之集體意識，同時，兼具自然、人文與心靈的宏觀格局，含容文化、歷史和哲學之有機架構。期望以文人三向的融貫統攝，延伸藝道美學之會通整合，開展靈動思惟的創造活動，使得超逸思想理路、正向觀念演繹，呈現高度自覺的展覽及風格。

基於對「藝道美學」的思想審度，長期透過自我審視與精神投注，希望藉由主體的意會、感通和靈覺，明確一切盡其在我、符應天地，揭示萬般發明本心、歸於自然，並以美在當下──含氣而應生，坦然面對內在的真實自己，究竟一探理想之生命藝術。因此，嘗試從「靈動思惟」之理路延展，持續探討東方超現實畫風的符號、象徵與意涵，以期盡心知性闡明靈度藝向：一、圖像式的人文蘊涵與思想光彩；二、自覺性的文化符碼與圖像意蘊；三、象徵型的感性內容與情境氛圍；四、精神化的形式歸向與本質還原。個人認為，所謂東方理想的藝術之道，應在於覺觀主體、悟明心性與自然合道，就此而言，有關「東方‧凝視」的藝術探索，自是符應體時用中、靈活西東，契合變通會適、神思制度。此一「文心雕龍‧十式」的創作觀，既是符應貫串古今兼顧中西，也似契合含空容有融貫統攝，儼如精神朝元與會相歸體，這種喻為「擬道化」的思考與實踐，旨在揭示主體內觀之心領神會，彰顯悟明自在的「靈智演藝」。

　　從藝術思想與表現形式的互動中，綜合主要展覽的內容概述，約略可知個人的藝術探索與發展趨向，其中顯然包括水墨精神性的思想源由、藝術靈動性的觀念演繹，以及東方超現實的風格表現。除了說明筆者藝術發展的脈絡、衍繹之外，也概述了主要風格型態的緣起、演變，同時，更是間接反映出「尊重己靈」的精神理想。基本上，筆者以符應主體心性的自然作用，將藝術信仰具體落實於「藝術／道理」，呈現出精神體驗的「情思／美感」，藉以反映生命存在的演變過程。在親身實證的自我追尋中，則是以「虛靜明白」的思想、理路，經由「盡心知性」的靜觀、內省，揭顯「盡性知天」的真理、實相，進而依循精神理念、藝術思想與創作實踐，予以具體而微的闡明、開顯，期望透過現實與超現實的互通性，呈現出「道理／藝術」之靈動思惟。

　　從以上敘述可知，所謂「自然‧合道」的究竟向度，如同「靈動‧契機」的變通會適，猶似「詩興‧明理」的本質還原，既屬東方人文蘊涵的覺觀思考，也是當代研學治藝之悟明辨析。有鑑於此，「理想藝術」並非在於虛擬演繹、異乎尋常，而是一種精神自然、藝術靈動，換言之，不是基於一種躁動心理、驚駭情緒，演示肆無忌憚的意識型態，而是在於映照主體的心靈狀態，一種活潑潑地「當機生息」，一種理所當然之「因緣成象」。而且，不是單一方向的邏輯思維，或是「物質性」之現實考量，而是還有其「精神性」的意蘊指涉，甚至於更深一層面內向探微，意即指涉一種「自然性」的神秘意謂，而若究竟終極存在之根本涵蘊，亦或可謂在於覺性悟道、顯見真際，此一喻為「境由心生」的思想理路，猶如對於「心物泯合」之理論闡明，其所揭示精神理想的藝術真實，應該就是不可思議之「靈動性」。

　　筆者長期投注於研究、探索與實驗之中，通過多年持續的研學、創發、明證，嘗試理解古今中外的藝術體系。在審視東西美學思想、藝術觀念，乃至創作表現經驗過程中，更加確立自主精神與超越意識的重要性，及其對於東方藝術（水墨）發展的影響性。並且，隱約覺察到諸多世界藝術類型，其中似乎存在某種靈活、生動的精神質素；也就是說，一種超越時空制約的共同屬性，那般難以令人全然置信，也無法為一般科學家所完全理解，即為穿梭古今、跨越西東之「全息系統」，其如同宇宙造化的「精神聯結」，猶似自然天地的「氣象演成」，可謂含容現象、能量、信息之「神秘場域」。關於此一宇宙自然的「全息系統」，我們從宋代理學家陸九淵的哲學思想，可知「吾心即是宇宙」的見解主張，然而，他不同於朱熹言「理」，強調探討宇宙自然的真理實相，而是偏重於人生倫理、心性修養，因此，在於「格物致知」層面，傾向於「心即是理」、「明心見性」。以藝術創作而言，無論「我心即宇宙」或是「宇宙即我心」，顯然都在寓意「藝術／道理」和「道理／藝術」，意為揭示藝術真理實相—「所以然」。從這個意義上講，個人認為，可以藉由「心即是理」加以探究，也就是通過道體（自然）神秘，彰顯主體（本性）神明，導啟本體（藝術）神靈，使得「天—心—物」一體，呈現出「言意象—契機」，「精氣神—明理」，以及「真善美—合道」，簡言之，即以一種自由的開放性心靈型態，經由內外世界溝通、交流、對話，體現出自在的超現實藝術風格；那麼，「靈機」扮演起「超感」連結，溝通於道樞、靈符、藝術之間。此處「靈機一動」的真正作用，實為召喚主體生命覺醒、精神復甦，既是促使活在當下理解「非常道」，也是引發恆持剎那詮釋「明明德」。基於這個觀念，從「觸機神應」時消解意識，自「良知妙顯」中活化精神；如此一來，所謂東方理想的藝術之道，也就在於自我淨化、靈魂昇華。這正如同《周易‧繫辭傳下》：「唯變所適」，是以靈動契機的美學思想，依自度合適的藝術觀念，建構一種個人化的創作模式。

整體而言，此一喻為格物致知的「藝術心學」，是個人自度合適的「觀象擬真」，為使避免因過於理想顯得簡略空疏，或趨於現實導致支離瑣碎，在藝術創造過程中，擬定偏重於靈動思惟的學理論說，概括而言，是以主體面對客觀的現實世界，營造一種藝術理想的精神天地，依視覺表象性的觀念指涉，具體映照內在心靈真實性。使得風格型態具有象徵性意涵，呈現出龍精神、玉性質、詩意蘊、夢現象、靈觀照。此外，透過道樞、靈符、藝術的互通幻化，顯示出視覺表象性（龍精神）、象徵性內涵（詩意蘊）、多義性特質（玉性質），以及動態性結構（夢現象）和心靈真實性（靈觀照），並且，藉由此一「集象合意」的思考與實踐，說明主觀藝術創作的內容蘊涵，而「唯變所適」體現出的精神靈動性，既是呼應「體—相—用」的宗教哲理真如觀，也似回應「覺—正—淨」的立體琉璃同心圓。（表6）

龍精神　玉性質　詩意蘊　夢現象　靈觀照

表6：《易經・繫辭下》：「唯變所適」

四、「觀象・擬真」的歸化實際

　　從中國藝術發展史論可知，歷代繪畫藝術的「變」與「革」，意謂「文化精神」的再生意義，指涉「藝術本質」之更新意識，綜觀史前時期繪畫藝術，如彩陶、岩畫、壁畫與地畫等，象徵東方獨特的文明曙光。夏商周三代時期繪畫藝術，如壁畫、青銅與帛畫等，有著精美璀璨的文飾風采；秦漢時期繪畫藝術，如壁畫、畫像石與畫像磚等，呈現龍騰鳳舞的形式意趣；魏晉南北朝時期繪畫藝術，如卷軸風格興起、壁畫型態隆盛，顯示文人與美藝的自覺；隋唐時期繪畫藝術，如精工細致人物畫，青綠、水墨山水畫，花鳥、畜獸畫的出現，以及石窟和墓室壁畫的發展，揭顯精神傳揚的盛世新聲。此外，五代時期繪畫藝術，如繁麗精整的人物畫、荊關董巨的山水畫，乃至徐黃異體的花鳥畫，標誌文化生命的承先啟後；宋代時期繪畫藝術，如精緻文雅的人物畫、精奇抒情的山水畫，甚或傳移精神的花鳥畫，顯明詩畫相映的精神況味，體現藝術生活之繼往開來；元代時期繪畫藝術，如尚「意」傳「情」的山水畫、托「物」言「志」的花鳥畫、抒「懷」寫「真」的人物畫，以及民間畫工的道釋壁畫等，呈現顯「道」明「理」的文人意向，儼然筆墨精神、元氣淋漓，其中題材風行的「四君子畫」，可謂應運而生、盛極一時；至於明代時期繪畫藝術，如繁榮興盛的山水畫、傳統的寫意花鳥畫，乃至向民間藝術回歸的人物畫，頗有與時偕行的大明風度；清代時期繪畫藝術，如「四王」吳惲、「遺民四僧」、「金陵八家」與安徽畫家，甚或「揚州八怪」和其他相關畫家，更有畫院畫家及西洋畫士、嘉道以後的繪畫形式，乃至民間木版年畫風格等，反映末代風流之繁殊異相；此後，由於西學東漸、求新求變，使得近代中國繪畫藝術發展，逐漸趨向於現實性的觀念演變，此一因應時代思潮的風格型態，雖說不乏鮮明的形式意趣，然而，從揚州畫派、海上畫派及嶺南畫派，甚或早期中國油畫的思想理路，約略可知中國藝術精神式微，無論「變古為今」的傳統研究、「變西為中」的現代探索，或是「變異為同」的當代實驗，形諸主體意向著實可見一斑。

由此看來，傳統中國繪畫藝術的風格型態，有其審「時」度「勢」之主體意向，或因應文化理想的變革與發展，或依循歷史進程之延伸和擴充，抑或映對哲學精神的架構及體系。然而，自從西方文明之急速引進，隨同科技導向的激越與影響，使得原本「變法維新」之企圖和目的，淪為意識演藝、物化思維，顯見主體渾然、意向不覺。有鑑於此，探討當代語境下的繪畫藝術觀，除了融貫似與不似、變與不變，以及異與不異，理應確認源於靈明自度，會通「覺－感－知」、整合「義－理－趣」，乃至統攝「形－神－靈」，以此明證「含道映物」、驗明「澄懷味象」，揭顯所謂藝道美學、靈動思惟，在於彰明覺觀主體、悟明心性，而其「靈明自度」的哲學思辨，喻為我之影響、法與無法，寓意美藝契合、思與非思。換言之，所謂東方理想的藝術之道，既須清楚文化背景、源流脈絡與形意雙全，也要明白歷史進程、心理結構和情思映對，同時，基於理以明事、事以顯理，探討精神境界與玄化秘境，避免成所作「識」和演藝為「物」。就此而言，筆者擬想依源於真正的生命實踐，說明依循自我追尋的主體狀態、精神理想的藝術境界，以及靈活運用的風格型態，並且，就有關階段發展的形式意趣，將其精要內容與象徵意涵，加以概略敘述如下：

（1）從傳統精神與源流研究，探討自然意會的美學內涵

即以傳統精神與源流研究，揭示自然意會的美學內涵，從中認識「哲理思辨」的比擬內容，同時，依源於東方道論和覺觀突破，融貫時間、空間、人間、事件及物象等面向。

（2）從現代思想與脈絡探索，探討人文感通的藝術特徵

即以現代思想與脈絡探索，呈顯現實生活的人文感通，從中理解「美學能靜」的寓意形式，同時，依源於禪宗心論和悟明創新，會通政治、經濟、社會、心理及宗教等面向。

（3）從當代觀念與理路實驗，探討心靈覺照的創作旨趣

即以當代觀念與理路實驗，映對主體生命的心靈覺照，從中體解「藝術會動」的象徵意涵，同時，依源於諸家氣論和顯見發展，統攝奇譎、雄渾、厚實、華麗及繁複等面向。

肆、「靈視・幻象」的理解與詮釋

有關「形象思維」的延伸論述，「象徵性」與「寓意性」之間，有其聯繫也有區別，共同之點在於借此言彼，前者由具體形式表現抽象內容；在現實生活中，人們常以約定俗成的方式，使「象徵體」和「象徵義」關係固定，成為較為確定之審美對象。後者由具體形式相似比喻而成，因此較少被完全固定下來。人們創造具有象徵性的形象，所運用的想像、聯想等種種能力，是經由長期審美實踐中獲得發展。 在藝術演化的創造過程中[4]，個人基於這種主觀之審美理想，嘗試以有機構成和系統整合，採取東方特有的靈動思惟，延伸宏觀、巨視之精神視野，期望突破舊有的框架與結構，表現廣大深遠之神思或想像。就此一觀點而言，當代文化學者余秋雨在《藝術創造論》書中提到：

對集體深層心理的開掘，使我們懂得藝術的普遍性意蘊，應該在自己的同胞的心靈深處去探測。就像歌德探出個浮士德，就像尼采探出個查拉圖斯特拉，我們的心靈只有在地底深處，才能發現使千萬人一起震撼的似有天心下頒的形象圖譜。[5]

4　王世德主編，《美學辭典》，53。
5　余秋雨，《藝術創造論》（臺北：天下遠見，2006），140。

由此觀之，這種喻為「天心」的形象圖譜，既是基於個體的精神體會，也是源於集體之文化自覺，此一「靈動天心」的象徵意涵，指涉主體（自我）之虛靈明覺，與一種心靈深處的智慧觀照。而集體深層心理之深入開掘，顯示出的是活之精神，演繹出的是有機生命，無論藝術的本源或美的本質，其中究竟之際儼如宇宙萬物之本體──「道」，因此，解明藝術創造的理想性意義，不只是呈露淺層表徵之欲望本能，而是揭顯深層意涵的存有本質；換言之，其所探究不應僅是在於自我滿足，而是應具有心靈深處之精神探測，也就是在於顯見覺性的本然系統，彰明神聖氛圍之生命「靈光」(Aura)，乃至體現藝術本身的普遍意蘊，並且，基於人類文化共同之精神理想，呈現出兼具靈性、智慧的真善美企圖。筆者在此就「靈視‧幻象」的理解與詮釋，依序探討有關：一、「靈視‧幻象」與精神性理論；二、「靈視‧幻象」與自覺性思考；三、「靈視‧幻象」與價值性實踐；四、「靈視‧幻象」與超現實畫風。

一、「靈視‧幻象」與精神性理論

　　承接上文所言，明確藝術創造的理想性意義，在於揭顯深層意涵的存有本質，彰明神聖氛圍之生命靈光，這正喻示藝術創造與生命實踐，有極為密切的互通關係，也就是說，其中隱含除距、去蔽與活性，呈顯覺照、正思和淨化，甚至揭示靈魂昇華之體驗過程。這種「神聖氛圍」的真正發生，主要在自我淨化、靈覺感通，以及觸機神應之時，作者以其主體自覺、親身經驗，賦予藝術獨一無二之精神品質。這般源於「誠心」、「正意」，符應「靈覺本真」、「發明自己」；如此緣起「格物」、「致知」，契合「自然感通」、「冥契造化」，可謂基於「尊重己靈」、「感物應性」，儼然《禮記‧大學》所言：「欲正其心者，先誠其意；欲誠其意者，先致其知，致知在格物。」

　　由此可見，喻為東方理想的藝術之道，具有心靈深處的精神探測，既可彰明神聖氛圍之生命靈光，也能揭示主體心性的情思美感，可謂道理清楚在於「真誠己意」，事實明白攸關「端正心術」，因此，明確主體自覺、感物應性，釐正思想理路、精神默契，即是寓意因「實在」而「存在」。此等精神性之思想理論，在於闡明「生命的藝術」，誠屬覺觀「道理的意義」，在藝術創造的理解上，不但是主體心性的內在修養，也是思想觀念之外在表現；審視此一道理自然、不容取代的意義，重探彼一藝術真實、無從複製的價值，使藝術自身映照主體心性，呈現出「靈動契機」的存在狀態。從哲理觀解的角度來看，所謂諸法實相無異、萬般緣起性空，意指一切皆為「擬真幻象」，而其之所以喻為「道法自然」，著實也就緣起我等「心變識現」，亦即綜合思維之心靈作用；同時，形塑現實不存在的象徵事物，營造超前想像之「未來情境」。

　　基於此，期冀透過可見的表象形態中，窺探到事物背後之事實真相，呈現出自然、人文與心靈之特殊蘊涵，以期顯明潛藏其間的「觀念生機」。因此，在有關意識、情感與精神的符號圖像，經由理性、感性和智性之融貫統攝，並加以自然地整合、會通及運用，營造出具有象徵蘊涵的美感意象。概括地說，對於當代多元化藝術的認知與覺察，加深體證到「靈視／幻象」的超現實性，增進對應人生現實、宇宙真相，以及生命實踐的哲思內省。以藝術創造而言，明確自己嚮往的「精神意向」，使其符應主體自覺之心靈活動，誠屬意味深長的「道理／自然」；而釐正自我實對的「藝術定位」，契合精神默契之意識演繹，實是理所當然的「真實／發展」。從這個意義上講，重探精神境界與玄化秘境，不但是一種清楚的思想見解，也是一種明白之觀念主張；換言之，對於「主體／心靈」的高度關注，即為獨立自主之精神取道；而對於「精神／意識」之積

極審度，則是「觀心自在」之思想理路，可謂顯見性靈、自然真實，甚且含涉道理、意義明確。（表7）

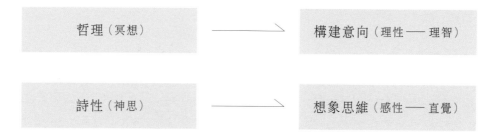

| 哲理（冥想） | → | 構建意向（理性——理智） |
| 詩性（神思） | → | 想象思維（感性——直覺） |

表7：精神境界與玄化秘境示意圖

就此而言，無論知識分子或是藝術學人，凡是基於生命意涵的高度關注，抱持文化理想觀、藝術文明論，乃至精神活化說等等理念，並以整體性觀照與全面地掌握，可謂具有堅定信念和正確見解，此即是說，若使清楚主體心性的自然作用，即可明白東方理想的藝術之道。因為，確知自我本性與自然道體，審度藝術思想和形式表現，即為源於「真」（誠摯）的精神理念；而具有所謂「國際眼光」，又能理出「中心思想」，也似緣起「善」（完備）的藝術思想。至於覺觀體證「活靈活現」，悟明顯見「真實自己」，誠屬呼應「美」（和諧）的創作實踐。此一「觸機神應」的靈活運用，演成「良知妙顯」之圓融觀解，可見思想與觀念的轉變歷程，顯示藝術文明的與時俱進，其中「真—善—美」的論述或言說，即為「道本自然」之具體呈現。因此，藝術本身是一種全息系統，風格形式是一種有機整體。

這般「真—善—美」企圖，是一種詩興蘊含之精神默契，在於喚起主體生命覺醒、精神復甦，不但引發哲思內省、揭示一心三觀，也似激越智性思惟、闡明靜極思動，儼然寓意本體思想朝向知識觀念，象徵心靈美學轉化視覺藝術。如果能以主體心性自然作用，在不因宗教理性的制約之下，又可回復天真朗現、不忘初心；那麼，無論「為人生而藝術」的標舉，或是「為藝術而藝術」之揭示，可謂既符應人性的呼聲，也契合靈智之企盼。在某種程度上而言，這不僅「現實／理想」層面如此，於「浪漫／憧憬」範疇亦如此，因為，彰明藝之為藝的「契機合道」，不但是對生命實踐的意識覺察，同時，也是就人之存在的精神覺照。

從文化溯源觀點來看，有關「靈視·幻象」與精神性理論，主要以文化特質、形上思維，以及美學內涵層面，作為問題思考與觀念延伸：

1.「靈視·幻象」風格的文化特質

基於東方主體性的思想理念，呈現具有當代理想之超現實畫風，研究中華特質的文化內涵，探討源於生命意識之歷史記憶，彰明隱喻道理真實的哲學精神。

2.「靈視·幻象」風格的形上思維

源自制心一處的智性思惟，明確心靈美學與視覺藝術之轉化，審視現實層面的變異現象，重探融貫統攝之「歸元本體」，映照自然精神、呈現「顯靈密趣」。

3.「靈視·幻象」風格的美學內涵

經由自度合適的哲思內省，顯示詩興蘊含之精神默契，從中釐清「東方前衛」的象徵意涵、審度「當代逸境」之精神內容，以期體現「靈覺本真」的圓融觀解。

　　從精神性理論觀點來看，無論「藝術／事實」的明白揭示，或是「自然／現實」之清楚顯見，著實在於主體自覺的觀念確立、生命意涵之思想理解，以及「本立道生」的精神體會。可見主體的靈明覺知（心），攸關客體（物）之內容意涵，這也說明精神自然、藝術靈動，就直覺與表現上而言，藝術事實如同自然現實，藝術本質猶似生命精神，而自然而然的「道理／存在」，顯明觀心自在之「真實／意義」，也就是說，「我—藝—道」的互通性運用，既需精神相應、本於自然，也要心思默契、合乎人事。當然，就哲理觀解層面予以解析，東方理想的「藝術之道」，可謂儼如天地造化自然生成，既是陰陽轉動、循環不息，也是隨機起用、任運而行，因此，解讀藝術靈動的「形式／事實」，不能否認道本自然之「內容／真實」，同樣地，「客體／意涵」的變與不變，也與「主體／自覺」有密切關係。

　　基於這個思想理路，「藝術靈動」的研究與探討，理應對自我本性有真正理解，明確心性契機、自然合道，釐正隨心所欲、因勢利導，進而彰明獨立精神、自由思想。以此詮釋所謂「生命的藝術」，顯然具有理想的「象徵性意義」，不但更符合哲學之本然系統，也易於找出自己的潛意識語言。如果從存在的角度審視，天地至精的人自有高度覺性，契機合道之藝必定靈動自然，主體自覺呈現出「靈通感應」，而藝術自明顯示出「生機勃發」，這也就是「妄盡還源」、「悟道顯藝」。以上敘述的一段文字，其中所講的「完全的人」，意指「身—心—靈」整合、「知—情—意」會通，著實喻為生命精神的重新覺醒，不但依道驗明「正身」（虛靈），也循理證得「真際」（實然），活出自己的「信心之美」，如此一來，覺觀「我—藝—道」的靈活性，即可彰明自我本性的關懷，同時，也能映照東方特質的文化思想，顯現當代表徵之藝術見解。（表8）

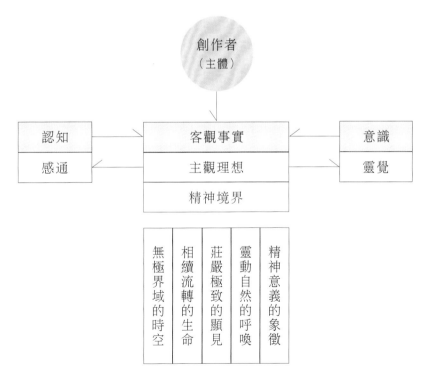

表8：自我本性的關懷（thought of the self）

覺觀「我─藝─道」的靈活性，對於日益式微的東方精神來說，指涉我等有必要就其核心意涵，予以整體性的審視與重探，從中認清所謂形上學與形下學，避免因為趨向過度思考、邏輯演作，或是渾然未覺、硬性因應，致使陷於高度制約的框架思維。也就是說，東方理想的「藝術之道」，實是符應中國形上學的美感意趣，其道理真實與科學認知誠然無涉，其藝術本質和理論實證沒有衝突；審視源流脈絡與思想理路，重探美學內涵和藝術特徵，意在契合主體心性的自然作用。此外，也是就其概念內容、精神意義與詮釋模式，作一種根本性的思索和探究，以期印證源流脈絡及思想理路。關於精神自覺的藝術探索，哲學理論對於「正身」、「真際」，只在形式層面上予以肯定，並不進一步有所驗明、證實，概括而言，不在事實上加以明確、釐正。哲學研究著重的是道理、本體，不強調處理事實、現象，因此，較為傾向於形上之思想範疇，而且，實際探討層面也與科學有別，主要關注抽象原理和普遍概念。在藝術創造過程中，筆者匯聚多元性的思想見解，擬以「靈動思惟」之精神理念，依「歸元整體」的思想理路，概述「文化生命」的自覺性、「美學生意」的精神性，以及「藝術生活」的創造性，從中清楚「思想生存」的價值性，明白「觀念生機」之意義性。循此精神理念的根本涵義，及其衍生之相關內容，探討有關「我─藝─道」的互通性；結合美術理論與創作實踐，揭示「靈視‧幻象」與藝術創作的關係，期望透過綜合理路之靈動性思惟，呈現出「契機合道」的超現實畫風。據筆者看來，具有象徵精神承載的藝術（水墨），理應基於自身所屬的傳統脈絡，呈現出獨特鮮明之現代型態；既須顯明源於東方的文化主體，也要展現緣起當代之藝術文明。從這個層面思考可知，喚醒主體精神回歸、心性意識顯明，對於高度覺性的藝術家們，誠屬至關重要的思想理路，尤其顯見「正道奇發」、呈現「藝術化境」，主要還是在於靈明的正向思惟。

　　自覺性思考如同靈動性思惟，揭示自我本性、自然道體，顯明精神活化、生命意涵，而且，攸關高度覺性、藝術理路，對於亟欲呈現「真─善─美」、擬想表達「情─理─法」，抑或試圖彰明「精─氣─神」，確實意義深刻、至關重要。因此，具有精神理想的藝術創作者，豈能絕然忽視、沉默以對，抑或渾然未覺、置身事外。殊不知，無論藝術本質的究原竟委，或是道理真實之正本清源，全然繫於我等自身的生命覺照，這不僅在於「主體／精神」如此，在於「心性／意識」亦如此。從藝術文明觀點來看，唯有融貫統攝之「會相歸體」，才可體證「形式／自然」、「內容／真實」，也唯有完全的人的神秘體驗，才能靈魂昇華、人格光明，因此，主體自覺揭示客觀的理想性，而精神體會呈顯主觀之靈動性，理解隱含其中的箇中奧妙，即為通往「契機合道」之最佳途徑。

　　從歷史演成之觀點來看，有關「靈視‧幻象」與自覺性思考，主要以發展潮流、理論建構，以及當代功能為思考層面，作為問題思考與觀念延伸：

1.「靈視‧幻象」風格的發展潮流

　　基於「本立道生」的精神體會，透過自覺性思考之研究理路，清楚自身所屬的傳統文脈，明白觀念演變之現代型態，並且，靈活呈顯自度合適之藝術探索。

2.「靈視‧幻象」風格的理論建構

　　期望依循主體的精神意向，覺觀「我　藝─道」之靈活性，使得藝術符應生命本真、「靈動天心」，契合情思美感、「覺照人間」，顯見真誠內在、「發明自己」。

3.「靈視‧幻象」風格的當代功能

　　源於一種潛意識的真我探索，運用「契機合道」之研究進程，以「自然之理」明確自主超越，依「人文

之情」表達社會關注，因「心靈之法」顯示智性思惟。

三、「靈視‧幻象」與價值性實踐

　　透過自覺性思考的研究與探討，可以審度文化理念和藝術問題，而藉著美之獨特性的心靈感知，則能夠理解主體存在及思想境界；同時，在生命所依存的世界當中，也可基於多發性的意向開展，彰明生命本元之神秘能量。這種神秘能量的具體呈現，是緣起諸多因素的集合構成，是彼此融會、互通之有機整體。此即是說，身體、情感、心理與精神的能量匯聚，使我們感覺到真正超越和解脫。從中確知自由的意識形態、自適的情感現象，以及自然的精神狀態；由此觀之，基於完全的人之覺性明德，以獨特自我的內在靈視，依「擬道化」之藝術品味，透現「靈自在」的高尚企圖，觀照高度和諧之生命本然。在某種程度上而言，這也就是靈昭明覺、契機合道，呈顯自然而然的藝術理想，因為，其既符應純粹形而上的研究對象，也揭顯精神性論說的真際實然，同時，反映一種道理真實之核心意義。從藝術的精神性觀點來看，畫家、詩人的靈感意興和自然表現，與其人格氣質及精神修養，有著極為密切的互通關係，意即藝術精神的靈動體現，正須由作者自己之審美觀念，經由精神識解以建立思想取道。其中含攝靈動的美感與意蘊，既是詩興和靈心之精神交會，也是主客兩忘、言相俱遣，可謂兼具精神默契與意識隱合。儼如一種超心理學的觀念寓意，抑或一種超感官知覺之思想學說，這種觀念寓意和思想學說，是來自主體之聯想、思緒、夢幻，乃至靈感映出的精神意境。此一含蘊生命本質的終極經驗，即為一種契機合道之真正「實在」，其既揭示了人類存在的象徵意涵，也呈現出身心靈層面之整體實相。從以上敘述可知，探討這種因「實在」而「存在」，需要清楚「美學／內涵」的概念意義，明白「藝術／特徵」之思想理路，其實，所謂喻為純粹的美學經驗，也就是超乎利害之生命意涵，而寓意超然的藝術現象，亦即為無功利目的精神導向；換言之，純粹美學經驗是源於生命覺醒，而超然藝術現象則是緣起精神復甦，可見對精神靈動性的高度關注，有如對藝術自然化之積極審度，其問學之道解與不解，就在是否明白立體琉璃同心圓。（表9）

表9：精神靈動性與立體琉璃同心圓

　　在藝術創造過程中，如此絕對精神的全能體現，是通過意會、感通的階段推展，進而演成主體自覺的意識範疇。就人化的自然而言，既是歷時經驗的「客觀／意識」，也是同時體驗之「主觀／覺察」，而其終極會通之處，不但在於感知「美的過程」，也在於證驗「會相歸體」，乃至覺照一種「無我之境」。如果從寬

廣的角度來看，是以超現實性的明顯發現，體證完全靈覺之潛意識流；由此可見，東方智慧的啟發與影響，闡明靈的主體、活之精神，呈顯覺性明德的現實目的，從中既可領悟生命的重新覺醒，也能理解精神之再度復甦，可謂顯見主體心性的自然作用，揭示悟道顯藝之理想意義。就此而言，令人感受到的「藝術／精神」，即為有機的靈動與自然，而對於覺察到的「道理／真實」，則是一種超逸之天工和清新。這也就是說，契合生命意涵的藝術理想，具有超然形上之道理真實，是體驗靈動而非觸目與驚心，是印證自然不在震懾和驚嘆。不可否認的事實是，美學思想與藝術觀念的演進歷程，終將因意識消融和情感轉化，顯示出道本自然之靈動昇華，使其原本分化的意識形態，成為有機融合之精神實然，讓此多元變異的意識執導，契合歸元整體之「靈覺本真」，此一超乎利害的藝術觀解，即為一種純粹的美學經驗，而意識演藝則未必如此。從這個意義上講，無論基於「靈性／還原」，或是係為緣起「智慧／統理」，其所呈現興會上揚的美學效果，都是具有生命意涵之審美創造，既是一種有機整體型態的系統性，也是一種主客精神互通之可能性。

值得注意的是，雖說當前東方美術與西方藝術，在一般現代人的心目中，似乎彼此地位平等，思想逐漸趨同、形式無別，見解日益融會、內容相近，可謂東西遇合、觀念呼應。不過，兩者在本質上仍然不無差異。以超現實繪畫風格而言，東方美術因宗教性思想啟發，說明傳統文化傾向在哲理內觀；西方藝術因心理學之觀念影響，顯示現代文化偏重於感官知覺。同時，在藝術的精神性與意義上，也映對其文化背景和心理結構。因此，如何從主觀意識的基本思考，經由進一步之觀念延伸，體認藝術形式的內含與外延，明確精神內容之象徵和意義。使得藝術原本單純的表象性，透過莊嚴的神聖性、極致的想像性，以及清淨的創造性，呈現出「契機合道」之真正意義，誠屬理所當然的東方思想。如此一來，基於主體自覺的心理機制，經由獨特自我之內在靈視，過渡到「無住生心」的超然覺觀，就是以近乎完全的人之思維模式，顯現出「無我／非思」的形上理喻，依源於東方智慧的文化理念，使得精神與思想重現一片曙光。

從哲學蘊涵之觀點來看，關於「靈視‧幻象」與價值性實踐，主要以藝術傾向、圖式表徵，以及創作觀念為思考層面，作為問題思考與觀念延伸：

1.「靈視‧幻象」風格的藝術傾向

符應「靈自在」的有機整體，契合生命存在之理想意義，揭示主客之間的精神實對，透過自然探秘、人文關懷和心靈究竟，彰顯「變異與歸元」的真實內涵。

2.「靈視‧幻象」風格的圖式表徵

基於一種獨特的純粹美學經驗，隱含喻為生命本質之終極經驗，以澄澈心靈洞悉「觸機神應」，依純粹意識顯明「良知妙顯」，呈現覺性通達、「盡心知天」。

3.「靈視‧幻象」風格的創作觀念

源自生命意涵的思想體會，呈現自我追尋之藝術理想，以智體理性研究「靈視意象」，依慧用解明探討「幻覺形態」，使得主體精神體悟、覺觀「潛意識流」。

四、「靈視‧幻象」與超現實畫風

當今藝術發展的多層面探索，既是源於「自我／知覺」的主觀形象，也似緣起「意識／衍異」之必然趨勢，因而顯示出極其多元化面向，但須加以注意的是，前述有關「靈覺本真」，意指生命覺醒的「靈性／還原」，也

是精神復甦之「智慧／統理」，這不僅對於主體本身而言，客體藝術亦復如此。從此點看來，這正說明自我淨化的精神覺照，攸關心和物之間的內在聯繫，寓意精神、物質互為因果，實是源自心靈活動的綜合作用。因此，我們不能否認：靈昭明覺的主體心性，是具有活化精神、可以創造形象，是含蘊自然機能、能夠顯見道源；由此觀之，「靈」活「運」用、演化生命，蘊含生生不息的精神動能，呈現化化不已之風格形式。從這個意義上講，宋代姜白石《續書譜‧情性》所言：「藝之至，未始不與精神通」，意為在於技、藝、道之間，存在一種我的精神性互通、連結，此說見於昌黎《送高閑序》，從這段文字之中，隱約也可理解靈活的形象與精神，就在直覺之思惟和運用。而透過主體情性的審視與重探，確知道理自然之意義和象徵，自是在於清楚藝術的精神性、明白創造之美學觀。此即是說，藝術發展逐漸朝向我的「精神性」，既是主體自覺的靈動意趣，也是藝術生活之自然興會，況且，理解藝術與精神的互通關係，也能導引創作意旨契合「真實性」。

所謂「靈動思惟」的精神理念，即在明確「創造性」的自然功能，這正如前面說過的，在於清楚藝術的精神性、明白創造之美學觀。從哲思內省的觀點來看，「思」與「想」在融會貫通之後，尚須「心」與「理」的真實因應；使得「性」與「道」的自然靈活，達到「心」與「行」之運用無間。此一「感而遂通」的象徵意涵，本是《周易‧繫辭傳上》明理之喻，用以形容極其幻化的「易之神妙」，寓意超導之「靈的奇譎」，其意即是：「易無思也，易無為也，寂然不動，感而遂通……」，藉由「感而遂通」的如實體會，以「易之神妙」彰明歷程即真際，解析「道理／藝術」的蘊含意義；依「靈的奇譎」揭示功能即實體，闡明超感知覺之「精神／體驗」，進而採「變通會適」的觀念寓意，概述主體心靈之「唯易思想」，在藝術創造中的「靈感作用」。不難理解，當前藝術家對於「潛意識流」的反應，猶如對於「靈覺本真」之理解，至於東西二方有其異同、各行其是，然而，我們也可就其本質等量齊觀，換言之，將其視為相互融合的潛在成份，屬於同一有機的藝術體系。東方超現實主義之「心靈／真實」，可以看作整體的恆定（靈化）面向，西方超現實主義之「心理／現實」，可以看作整體的變動（異化）面向。東方哲學思想的積極、肯定層面，可謂一種活的精神之靈動演化，一種「體─相─用」的自然顯明，此一精神自主的唯易觀，基本上，與同時性理論有相通之處。那麼，所謂理想化的藝術活動，不再只是唯物論、唯心論，而是傾向於「究竟現實」之唯易觀，因此，這種精神、意識的互通性，儼如具體世界和抽象世界的關係，概而言之，其或可喻為：「生命型態─萬象唯心經，主體感通─繁華緣夢生。」（表10）

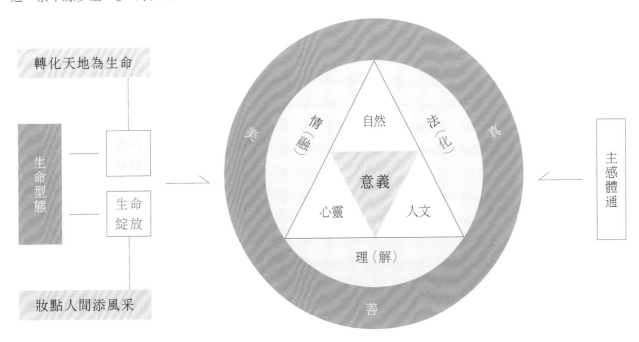

表10：主體感通──繁華緣夢生示意圖

明確這種內在互通之主體狀態，可以清楚理想化的藝術活動，而釐正活的精神之靈動演化，也能明白有機整體的創作風格；從潛意識觀點來看，源自心靈顯現的藝術真實，映照主體之意識、情感和精神，呈現出生命形象的現實性，因此，主體自覺的精神意向，使得客體（藝術）靈活變化。如此一來，既可開展由意識消解、情感流動，召喚主體的生命覺醒，也能依道而進、循理而行，激越自我的精神復甦；甚至於藉由悟道顯靈、明理鑑真，使得「藝道合一」之理想實現，這般含容空有、超以世外，即為個人嚮往的「端正藝術」。二十一世紀的今日，在這全球化思潮之下，東方文化的更新或再生，顯示對「集體／原型」的意識與關注，而當代藝術的多層面探索，呈現對「原型／本我」之覺察和重視。這也說明「潛在性」的真正意義。可見靈動思惟的精神理念，乃是基於內在之合目的性，揭示隱藏其中的神秘引介；此一靈活創造的藝術思想，揭示生命意涵的「本質／要素」，實屬一種東方化之「美學／意義」。而且，以此映對藝術自明的思想境界，亦可確知理想的精神內容、實質形式。就自覺與異化而言，新世紀人類文明的真正理想，顯然在主體的自覺和心性之顯明，此一探索攸關迷悟之思想解讀，也是藝術創作關鍵所在，因此，這種靈的主體自然演化活之精神，實是心靈科學與智慧哲學的發展指向。故嚴密地說，那非得是「心思默契」不可，而喻為生命本然的明白顯見，在於靈昭明覺之「自性實現」，這既是一種個性化之精神追求，也似一種潛意識的真我探索。在形而上美學的意義層面，既是促成主體的精神自覺，使其朝向複數性之思想延伸，也是導引個人信仰的藝術創作，逐漸契進「擬道化」之理路發展。

　　從藝術創作之觀點來看，關於「靈視‧幻象」與價值性實踐，主要以積極意義、實驗精神，以及表現方法為思考層面，作為問題思考與觀念延伸：

　1.「靈視‧幻象」風格的積極意義

　　明確「擬道化」的藝術實踐，呈現自然生動之靈活形象，透過源於精神自主的「莊嚴理想」、緣起意識超越之「極致現實」，回歸生命本然的「清淨自性」。

2.「靈視‧幻象」風格的實驗精神

　　釐正「唯易觀」的超現實畫風，以直觀揭示純粹之意識形態，依直覺呈現淨化的情感現象，用直心顯明超然之精神狀況，呈現出超感知覺的「精神／體驗」。

3.「靈視‧幻象」風格的表現方法

　　透過「有機體」的系統整合，依藝術創作實際需要，採用多元化之媒材技法、多樣式的畫面構成，以及多義性之主題內容，顯明「道理自然」的意義和象徵。

伍、新文人精神與新人文精神

　　洞悉貫通傳統、現代與當代的「義理」，即可超越有限時空、意識和界域之藩籬，使得東方水墨可以精神回歸，當代藝術能夠靈動顯見；在明確「道理」、「事實」意義之下，朝往靈覺真際、感通實處的正向發展，理解水墨本身是一種有機生命體，是源於主體心性之自然開顯。如果此一靈動思惟的觀點成立，那麼，我們也就能更加地確信：東方藝術（水墨）能夠契機合意、映照靈符，當代藝術可以順理應心、符合時代。如果「水墨／藝術」蘊含新人文精神，那必然是嶄新的華夏文明、震旦氣象；如果「藝術／水墨」象徵新文人精神，那必然是蘊含靈動、詩興、自然的特質。可見水墨性格的如實顯明，就是主體心性之精神自覺，能夠

確立這種精神自覺，即可開展個人未來的藝術理想。有鑑於此，審度東方學人與藝術觀念，除了確立主體精神和創意構思，也是對時間（風）、場域（土）、主體（人）、事件（情）、物質（藝），做整全而合理的積極關注；綜合前述，筆者認為理想藝術在於激越客體、使得「精神活化」，藝術理想在於悟出主體、顯明「活化精神」，換言之，在於揭示主體心性的自然而然，呈現藝術旨趣之契機、明理、合道。（表11）

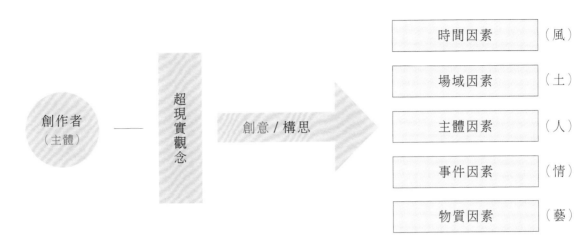

表11：東方學人與藝術觀念示意圖

　　而喻為養正導和的水墨意義，則因著主體的生命覺醒、精神復甦，啟發藝道之意會、感通、靈覺，如此一來，不但符應輝煌其神、中華之魂，也契合時空場域、自我定位。假使能夠「虛靜」、「明白」、「知道」，深切體認「道理／藝術」、「藝術／道理」；那麼，水墨的「魂兮歸來」將為時不遠。此時無論就東方精神而言，抑或以當代意義來談，會歸於是的藝術之道，儼如契合體現本身、顯明性德。在此，筆者就水墨、墨彩、彩墨的物質理解，擴展至藝道美學之精神詮釋，並且，以個人對臺灣、中國、東方的客觀認知，延伸到靈動思惟之主觀解讀，進而援引生命意涵的簡明論說，概述自己信仰之「觀象擬真」。依此明確東方理想的藝術之道，既在於彰顯靈的主體、導啟活之精神，也在於映照天地境界、契應文化本源，以期顯見究竟真實的靈動自然。因此，其美學旨趣是精神朝元的，其藝術歸向是生機活化的，可謂兼具虛靜、實動的哲理寓意，抑或唯易象徵之「含章可貞」；同時，以喻為「興中意會」的東方學人，淺介「感時契機」之藝術觀念。茲分別條列、循序說明如下：

（一）古今精神轉化・中西思想匯通

　　這個世紀東西文化的交流、溝通與對話，已是一個不可迴避的問題意識。無論是從生活理念的價值觀層面，或是自藝術探索之精神性範疇，我們都得予以全面審視、整體考量，重新確立文化理想、精神高度，以期增長民族的自信心。因此，透過古今精神的靈動轉化・中西思想之自然匯通，將現實與理想融合在一起，並且，用真誠的心、感人之靈，具體呈現於生命覺醒的創作實踐，自是可以顯見契機、明理、合道之藝術理想。

（二）結合多元文化・創造民族特色

　　若欲使得震旦氣象再現、華夏文明復甦，需要具有前瞻性的文化理念，一方面需要明確集體的文化自覺，以「正本清源」之思想理路，從中審視「東方精神」的真實蘊涵；另一方面則應釐正個體之精神體會，依

「主體心性」的自然作用，致力重探「當代意義」之真實呈現。基於文化理想的藝術探索，源自精神高度之智性思惟，進而透過多元文化的融會、結合，創造具有民族特色之藝術風格，才能真正符應靈明開權、契合智慧顯實。

（三）反映生活現實・傳達時代見證

　　藝術探索映照東方主體、顯明當代生活，可謂喻為道理真實的「根本所在」，而基於「本立道生」的思想理路，揭顯生命奧祕之風格型態，實是契合藝術文明的「魂兮歸來」。因此，明確主體心性的自然作用，釐正靈動思惟之精神理念，攸關藝術依道而運、循理而行。此一喻為東方智慧的真正意義，既在於清楚集體的文化自覺，也在於明白個體之精神體會，這正使得藝術發展的理想開顯，不但自然地反映生活現實，而且也是靈活地傳達時代見證。

（四）根源生命體驗・呈現內在情思

　　藝術創作能否發揮具體作用，其中也有幾個層面值得關注，在師古（傳統）之中「取法」、於學今（現代）之際「明理」，重要關鍵在於悟性「合道」（自然）。因此，無論「讀萬卷書，行萬里路」的文化積澱，或是「外師造化，中得心源」的靈動感悟，除了探究主體精神、心性意識之外，也應該結合當代人的生活思想，依循自己獨特的審美追求，加以融貫發展、會通變化。其最終省思仍需回歸本真狀態，根源於自然的生命體驗，映照出真實之內在情思。

（五）理解藝術脈絡・顯示歷史真相

　　理解「正本清源」的主要意義，使得我們確立東方文化主體，釐定當代藝術演繹。而具有「傳統脈絡／現代型態」之精神共識，在藝術方向的思考上，必然能夠依循正面的探索理路，持續地由內深化、自然呈顯。也就是說，在審度自身藝術脈絡中清楚溯源，在顯示歷史真相意義上明白探祕。由於明確「契機合道」的終極目標，對於藝術（水墨）之變革與發展，不但可以更為自主且超越，也將因此顯得積極而肯定，未來自是會有較為理想的創造結果。

（六）感應現代氛圍・探索心理結構

　　把藝術作為一種「精神理想」追求，確實可以從中獲得很多啟發，然而，值得注意的問題是，藝術如同科學探求現實真理一樣，從事藝術與科學也有同樣的問題；也就是說，既不能擺脫現實意識的箝制，也無法捨棄客觀認知之影響。因此，難以全面地觀照自己、整體地把握世界，發揮浪漫之人審美的主動性，遑論創造出映照真理之藝術品。確切而言，沒有這種「擬道化」的認識，自是不知何為「靈昭」感應現代氛圍，也不解何謂「明覺」探索心理結構。

（七）關懷人文自然・省思文明現象

　　文化不再只是表面思想的探求，更應積極關懷「人文・自然」之現象，省思文明衍生的種種問題，當今世界文化趨向多元發展，藝術並未因此益加進化、提昇，可見所謂「多元化」並不是異常催化，而是依道循理的多元並茂，藝術不再只是形式、觀念之延展，而是在於更多精神層面的關注。換言之，在於群體是否有文化自覺的認知，在於個體是否有精神理想之識見，而文化自覺的認知，實屬集體意識之思想體會；個體精神理想的識見，則是源自生命覺醒之靈動契機。

（八）綜觀天地造化・回歸性靈世界

　　對於藝術「擬人化」、「擬道化」的積極認識，使得筆者更加明白所謂「藝術／道理」，從中體會精神自主、綜觀天地造化，明白意識超越、回歸性靈世界。由此觀之，審美觀念反映創作者的心理變化，而精神

理念引導預期之自我完成。概而言之，面對階段性的生命經驗，是否整理記憶裡之人生事件，顯示出主體的靈性與智慧，對於藝術表現來說，由「主觀 → 客觀」、「被動 → 主動」的審視，到「形式價值觀 → 本質價值觀」之重探，說明從「現實因應」的意識超越，往「理想體證」之精神自主。

（九）主觀思維覺照・自我面目建構

　　智慧觀照呈現出一種心靈真實，即為本性圓融、和諧共生的自然狀態。此一思想理路，不但是主觀思維層面的意識覺察，也是自我淨化之精神覺照。以藝術創作而言，實是由理而解的形變、質化、神明，顯示出風格型態之靈動、詩興、自然。這般揭示自我面目的整體建構，既因藝術靈動而不同古人程式，也因精神自然而不像西方樣式，可見理想藝術的研究與探討，應該更多從智性思惟上予以明確釐正，而不僅是從形式表現、筆墨技法上面來看。

（十）國際宏觀視野・地方本土情懷

　　時代的意識丕變、審美的觀念衍異，對於多元文化的真正價值，總是存在著不同的解讀，因此，有關藝術文化的重新思考，理應回歸東方主體、經由智慧觀照，既要開展國際的宏觀視野，也須關注地方之本土情懷，同時，積極正視攸關存亡的文化生機。當前，東方「精神」可否與時俱進、因勢利導，實在難以驟然判定；當代「意義」能否否極泰來、應運而生，也似無法即時辨明。不過，從現實因應往理想調適的轉化過程，即為一種自我淨化與精神超越。

（十一）超越事物表象・思索深層意義

　　東方水墨是一種獨特的繪畫媒介，除了具有溝通內在之情意功能，也隱含「靈覺本真」的高度作用。這種如同「以心印心」的特殊型態，是在於自然而然中「開權顯實」，此一深層意義的思索與探究，既需要清楚自我之身心世界，也需要明白對象的真實狀態，因此，可說是以主體心性的精神體會，重探「藝術本質」之積極意義。概括而言，這般近乎理想的藝術意識或覺察，可以超越事物表面現象、深入對象內在層面，探悉到隱藏其中之真理實相。

（十二）法理之外傳情・真善之內存美

　　這種「靈覺本真」的高度關注，猶如「以靈見靈」之精神體會，是來自於內在真實的自我呈顯，並不刻意強調觀念之對立與矛盾，也不全然著重概念的集結和統合，而是較為傾向意念之融貫及會通。此一義理與旨趣，是心靈和意識之間的相依互存，也是語言圖像意義之靈活應用，而且，藝術之法（結構）、自然之理（規律）的外在顯現，傳達一種「契機合道」的人生之情，換言之，在科學之真（理智）、宗教之善（理性）的內在層面，其實也存在一種藝術之美（感性）。

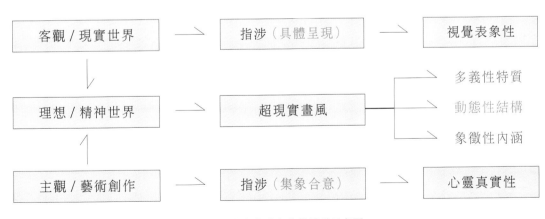

表12：自度合適與美學體系示意圖

陸、結論

由於對藝術的精神性之體會，更加確認自度合適與美學體系，筆者嘗試跳脫傳統的思想框架，走出個人既定之觀念侷限，不再執著於原本的風格制約，而是以精神蘊涵與內容意義，作為現階段主要的表現型態。概括而言，從「文化生命」、「藝術生活」、「思想生存」、「觀念生機」，以及「靈動生意」概念中，覺察到一切緣起的藝術現象，無論種種精神性的演繹，抑或諸般物質化之紛呈，其實都是因心靈與意識的相互作用，呈現出一種自在、自得的靈動「顯象」，只要經由主體心性的精神覺照，則能使其隨緣、任運的自然「還生」。

這也就是說，對於超現實畫風與生命的覺醒，理應呈現新人文之精神本質，體現出理想性的藝術意義。就道、心與氣同為存在範疇來講，所謂「天地與我並生」的整體性，抑或「萬物與我為一」之系統觀，其實是基於一種主體自覺，排除障礙性的自我意識，回歸道德人之生命本然，殊不知符應生命意涵的藝術創作，並非僅只依靠理智判斷、自我試煉、或者意識操作；只是侷限於大腦功能層面，聚焦在極其瑣碎的事務之上；只是受制於心理作用層面，以致缺乏整體審度與全面掌握。

基於此，筆者認為釐正主體自覺之思想理路，誠屬攸關真理意義的主觀詮釋，此等不偏不倚之精神覺照，即為一以貫之的「中庸之道」。因此，關於現實與超現實的思想互通，有待我等對於視域融合的客觀理解，這種幻覺形態的靈活意趣，如同「含空容有」之擬化精神，猶似「變通會適」之唯易思想，既是源自天啟喻示的靈感創發，也是緣起人生觸類之經驗體悟；在某種程度上而言，除了是一種體時用中的「藝道美學」，更是一種任運西東之「靈動思惟」。

附註說明：本文參考筆者博士論文與期刊專述，並從中選取整理和摘錄引用。

博士論文：《從「靈視、幻象與潛意識流」—探討彩墨超現實畫風的符號、象徵與意涵》（臺北・國立臺灣師範大學美術研究所文獻）

期刊專述：〈「靈思百度・活化理路」—從當代語境談東方繪畫藝術觀〉於《工筆畫期刊》第45期（臺北・中華民國工筆畫學會出版）

Thinking and Practice in Using the Doctrine of the Golden Mean to Experience Change

Article | **Lee Yi-han**

Stages of autonomous spiritual development

The philosophical observation of "aesthetics of artistic principle" not only relates to the aspirations to "inspirational thinking," it also influences the "spiritual height" of awareness. The focal point of this research is to showcase personally confirmed "awareness" through the "subjective self-awareness" of inspirational opportunities, and reflect the "enlightenment of artistic display" as evidenced through personal experience.

The leisurely life images and beautiful memories of the past, not only enrich one's personal experience of nature, but also highlight one's own cultural bearing, which is to say art matches subjective spiritual awareness. Through the clear establishment of the "spiritual" it is therefore easier to understand "art as reason."

Based on personal life experience, the writer explains the subjective state of self-pursuit, the spiritually ideal art world, type of artistic exploration and the stages of artistic development. Other than the painting enlightenment period (1959-), this experience is divided into five periods.

Traditional foundation period (1969-)

This period was when I started learning painting. In terms of learning the focus was on traditional ink concepts and Western painting knowledge. The learning process was step-by-step and evolved gradually, from brushwork, to copying and method arrangement. From these, we can gain a rough understanding of quality and appearance, which gives us a brief experience of the look and reality of "consciousness."

Nature quest period (1979-)

This period relates to research undertaken at college. In terms of learning the focus was "writing shaped matters," "probing fun," "searching and creating." I emphasized media techniques and blending scenes. The main thinking emphasized "foreign teacher good fortune," "memorization by heart," and "entire spirit and body." The hope was that through objective awareness of "images of good fortune," I could understand the subjective appeal of "wonderful nature," and experience the spirituality of "life vitality."

Cultural focus period (1997)

This period was a stage in my master's degree research. In terms of learning, the focus was on "the sources of ideas," "ancient style and new features," and "era image." I emphasized the exploration of format structure and creative artistic concepts. The main artistic thinking focused on "true and ancient," "soul cultivation," and "correct education, peace guidance." The hope was to use a comprehensive awareness of "Eastern aesthetics" to better understand the true meaning of "artistic creation and the concept of "cultural self-awareness."

Spiritual period (2006-)

This period was a stage in the research for my doctorate degree. Learning focused on "spiritual and visual imagery," "illusory forms," and "stream of consciousness." We emphasized the exploration of theme content and sixth sense responses. The main artistic thinking focused on "calling for the East," "ink vitality," "inspirational soul calling." I hoped through the subjective understanding of "moral enlightenment quodis arcana," to understand the ultimate intention of "spiritual awareness," and experience the profound secrets of "inspirational nature."

Self-existence period (2012)

Despite calling this the self-existence period, as a stage in the research of my own future style, it also connects to the past, continued into the present and develops into the future. In this period, I focused on "variation phenomenon," "returning ontology," "epiphany and interest." I focused on final definitions and exploring self-pursuit. The main ideas emphasized being "inspirational heaven's heart," "world awareness" and "self-invention." I hoped through awareness of "solemn ideals," to understand the intention of ultimate reality, in order to experience the subjective "pureness of nature."

From here, it became clear that natural truth is not fixed, unchanging, or conscious, but is rather a life concept that transcends transitory beauty. In the meantime, artistic faith is not a perceptual delusion, or a rational insistence, but an extension of reason. As such, whether natural truth or artistic both originate in life itself and inspirational use, appearing naturally with subjective temperament, based on spiritual experience and rational evidence. As for the interplay of art, the universe and life, it proves the sense, understanding and telegnosis of existence, while also confirming the cleanness, freedom, and release of life and even the self-appropriateness of life experience. As for "art/reason," it is self-confirmed "awareness" and self proven "enlightened art" that displays the "solemn nature" of Eastern aesthetics and shows the "understanding of justice" in modern art. By extending this concept, we can say that the nature of subjective temperament is self evident. Moreover, spiritual self awareness is the inspirational function of subjective spirit, and also the natural function of inspirational awareness. Therefore, spiritual self-awareness is a barometer of sense, perception and rationality. Artistic ideals are the hyperlink between opportunities, reason and coming together. In this way, reason is revealed as part of the human mind and art is grounded in reason.

Essence of spirit, creation of beauty

During the rapid changes undergone by modern art, the exploration of artistic ideas and expressive forms has been of key importance. As a creator of art, "artistic meaning" should be made clear. I adhere to the spiritual ideal of "respecting one's own soul" to evaluate the self-awareness of subjectivity and focus on the spirituality of artistic ideals. In another words, after a high level of philosophical introspection, we can gain a better awareness of our inner spiritual state and by concentrating can see the personal and innate truth of life. At the same time, based on the origins of Mankind, we re-explore the nature of subjective temperament to clarify the meaning of artistic creation. In this way, we can confirm the real objective of "artistic self-explanation" is spiritual nature and artistic inspiration expressed through philosophical thinking, in order to understand Eastern spirit, interpret modern meaning and experience why reason and truth are clear. Based on this concept, as part of the process of subjectively interpreting artistic creation, it should be possible to confirm the essential restoration of "poetic mood, reason," reflecting the interplay of nature, culture and spirit. Here, the author focuses on nine of my major exhibitions, and explains the related artistic thinking and practice, in the hope of showcasing the "flash of spiritual inspiration" through observation, imagination, and experience. From selection, grouping and performance, we display the "creation of beauty" of the spiritual realm. We can feel and evaluate- "the inner definition," so we can observe and manifest- the external "image," so this becomes an artistic phenomenon of spiritual and artistic conception. The summary is as follows.

"Eternal Tai Lu" series period (1984-)

The "Eternal Tai Lu" series of works simply attempt to use the expressive language of traditional aesthetics to create literati landscape scenes to convey a spiritual creative appeal, showcasing a world of ideas that symbolizes "the unity of Heaven and Earth." This series represents not only the coming together and research of natural scenery, but also the observation and discussion of spiritual tolerance and experience that had a deep and profound impact on my art. For example, my large creative forms in the 1980s were inspired and influenced by this period. The creation of the "Eternal Tai Lu" series, focuses on scenes from Taroko Gorge in Hualien. Scenery in the area is openly displayed, the main features being beautiful valleys, clear rivers, and beautiful clouds, rocks and lush forests. It is replete with the beauty of nature and culture.

"Moon World Illusion" series period (1988-)

The "Moon World Illusion" series of works mainly uses an expressive method that combines scenery and emotion, with the implied meaning of natural scenery laid bare. In other words, these not are only a formal exploration of objective reality but also a testament to the content of personal spirit. For a long time, the images of the Moon World have remained with me. In 1988, I traveled to a wonderful place of illusion hoping to see everything, the boundless and mournful scenes. What I saw in front of me were gray-white mountains of mud, isolated pavilions, barren withered jujube, a place almost barren of people, another amazing scene from Taiwan. Afterward, whenever the author recalled what he saw, he was moved by its desolation which he described as a desert and engendered feelings of melancholy and depression. The feeling was difficult to describe. Perhaps, this honest response incited an indescribable excitement, namely the inspirational interaction of subjective state of mind and the external world, leading to the natural emotional connection of scenes and emotions.

"Taiwan - image" series period (1992-)

Taiwan's traditional emphasis on ancient Chinese culture and thinking and its connection to national identity, or the extension of historical memory were energetic and unforgettable. If the boundless Pacific Ocean offsets the beautiful scenery in Taiwan, then the grandness of nature highlights the uniqueness of this "treasure island." I find Taiwan's nostalgic local customs and practices, and resplendent culture intoxicating. This is part of the island's warm and tolerant image. Today, modern Taiwan has 400 years of history, but has always embraced artistic essence, and that extends into its vision of the future, as seen in the spiritual grace of Taipei 101. It stands as a symbol for the times of civilization as it proudly towers into the clouds and looks down on the prosperity of modern society. In this context, I seek to take fortitude and toughness blended with a proactive and positive character, in using Eastern intelligence symbolizing brightness and spirit, and continue to guide the inspirational art that informs Taiwan's self-awareness.

"East/ New Image" series period (1996-)

Regarding artistic thinking about "the millennium," I was deeply sad and happy at the same time, whereas the "post-modern" situation causes me psychological anxiety and confusion, which is unexpected and about which I have mixed feelings. As such, the author focused on "spiritual heritage from past to present and the blending of Chinese and Western thinking" as the main focus of exploration in this period. In the meantime, I followed the artistic styles, forms and techniques of Eastern spirit to express the philosophical ideas on different cultures. I hoped through the ideal of spiritual interplay, to bridge the gap between Eastern ink art and Western painting. In other words, I sought to free ink from the confines of materialistic thinking and embrace spiritual awareness. From high cultural ideals, we extracted and concentrated the essence of Chinese traditional ink art and after a complete evaluation and re-exploration, moved in the direction of artistic transformation, showcasing continuity from ancient to modern times and asking why Chinese and Western art should be separate.

Vientiane Heart Sutra series period (2000-)

This proactive effort to combine religion and art has the symbolic meaning of philosophy and spiritual wisdom. In other words, individuals desperately want spiritual understanding and the intimate relationship of awareness and artistic principle reflects the interplay of spirituality and awareness. In terms of image and symbol expression, it is the autonomy of silence that expresses the existential sense of self-introspection. From here, it discloses the appeal of tranquility. For this, "telegnosis/understanding" remain important elements in the art. As for the overall style and content, I have gradually moved in the direction of spiritual outcomes. The author deliberately creates crystal clear visual effects, which highlight the creative style of changes in form and quality, so the work contains meditative-like spiritual inspiration and expresses the wonder of mysticism. This transition and transformation to surrealist painting style can be traced to the inner consciousness and awareness.

"Prosperous Destiny and Dream" series period (2002-)

From a certain perspective, this series is covert art and was also a turning point in my personal creative history. As such, the ideas and spiritual meaning in this period are not only more clearly move in the direction of idealized art, but are also imbued with surrealist style. In terms of artistic exploration, it differs from my earlier emphasis on form and technique. Because ink art is a special Eastern medium, I wanted to extend its traditional experience, but I didn't want to adapt the same extreme focus on compositional integration and completeness as in earlier series. From the form and content of this period, one can see that ideas I habitually used in the past disappear. Although this series lacks the stability and focus of the past, it contains more subjective imagination and expression. The ink art I produced at this time is a "fusion of Chinese and Western" elements. I even actively extended my creative thinking and explored multimedia.

"Virtual Modern Lotus" series period (2004-)

After 2004, my works focused on not only subjective scenarios, the creative method evolved from changes in form and substance to hiding technique in formlessness. In this context, what might appear to be easy image features that simplify the efficient design of the entity, no longer pursues spiritual expression but allows viewers to associate with super "nature." This illusion-like transformation of symbols and images is the convergence of visual effects on spiritual meaning. This allusion to hidden expressive types indirectly explains my personal intensity and turmoil. Such spiritually-oriented transformation and expression differ from the previous rigid adherence to reason and rigor. Indeed, the approach is more free and open, and in terms of thought more diverse and flexible, imbued with much more strange and illusory uncertainty. One could perhaps characterize it as an alternative type of Zen meditation.

"Spiritual Vision, Illusion" series period (2008-)

This series involved the production, use and experience of "Spiritual Vision, Illusion" and its relationship to artistic creation. I took spiritual vision image, illusory forms, and stream of consciousness to explore "real" constructs and "virtual" judgments, which evolved into surreal metaphysical scenes, displayed as a reflection on the essence of art. Moreover, from research into traditional and classical painting we understand what is meant by "aesthetic calm." In modern and romantic creative expression, we know what is mean by "art moving." At the same time, we see there exists an eternal spirit that runs through tradition, classicism, modernism and romanticism and this provides us with a comprehensive understanding of the inner essence of Eastern ink art and Western art. In terms of modern meaning the hope is to find a common spiritual meeting point through high minded reflection and in the process reveal the towering sense of the virtual way and the basic understanding of "telegnosis."

The aesthetic perspective of inspirational thinking refers not only to restoring the essence of "poetic creation, reasoning," it is basically based on the rationalism of Eastern Taoism, health and life in the Zen theory of the mind, and the changing theories of Qi propounded by other doctrines. This is used to evaluate aspects of subjective knowledge and re-explore the true meaning of artistic awareness. Furthermore, by viewing the language alienation of modern thought from the real natural principles of

Taoism, which is to say art itself, phenomenon and application, we can identify many extended meanings and connections, thereby avoiding the improper use of knowledge and language. As such, at the same time as we come to understand that traditional paths and modern concepts are clearly in line with the self-pursuit of life realization, the artistic exploration of true individual spirit becomes apparent and that allows us to interpret the stylistic symbolism of "inspiration life meaning." This idea emphasizes the "aesthetic calm" of Eastern thinking, which highlights the inspirational function of subjective spirit. The modern desire for "art moving" seeks to stimulate natural conscious awareness, which has philosophical loftiness, emotional breadth and spiritual depth. Overall, the thinking of art's "physical knowledge" seeks to clarify the spiritual meaning of new culture and also reveal the emotional forms of the new literati. As for the inspirational thinking of artistic exploration, the insights of the wise men of the past sought to embrace the spiritual hopes of nature, culture and spirituality, highlighting in the process the cultural prospects of eras, peoples and societies, while also reflecting the symbolic content of subjective understanding, feeling and spiritual feeling. Because the spiritual concept of meliorism not only shows the importance we attach to life, but also our focus on cultural autonomy, artistic freedom and even subjective self-awareness, the profound mysteries of this spiritual civilization can be said to encapsulate a vision of Mankind that dovetails with that of the all-around cultured.

From the "Ten Styles of the Literary Mind and Carving of Dragons" - Discussing the visual language and characteristics of modern ink art (2017-)

Since receiving orthodox painting training I have studied art for nearly 40 years. In that time I have not only been involved in the teaching and research of art, I have also regularly published academic paper and commentaries. On the day the world ended in 2012, the author received a Ph.D. from National Taiwan Normal University. From then on, I have had a deep understanding that the artistic path of the Eastern ideal is to be found in the natural application of the subjective temperament, which is the elimination of conscious and the rebirth of spiritual wisdom. I went on to more actively explore in the hope of revealing cultural meaning and artistic appeal through subjective awareness and wisdom. I later held the "Orient, Contemplation"- Lee Yi-han calligraphy and painting art exhibition at Sun Yat-sen Memorial Hall in Taipei. From the exhibition motif and the names of artworks, one can discern the focus is on absolute spirit and active awareness, which is also called "spiritual application." In other words, the life prototype of aurora, and the collective awareness of Chinese civilization not only can be traced back to the unique artistic spirit of the East, it is at the same time part of the grand pattern of nature, humanism and spirit, including the organic structure of culture, history and philosophy. The hope is to integrate the three literati traits, extend artistic aesthetics and develop inspirational thinking creation events, so that free and natural thinking together with positive concept deductions lead to exhibitions and style based on elevated awareness.

Based on the thinking of "artistic aesthetics, I have for a long time used self-evaluation and spiritual focus, in the hope of clarifying through subjective sense, feeling and telegnosis that everything up to me is in accordance with Heaven and Earth, revealing the original intention of invention in a return to nature, and embrace beauty in the moment - calmly face my real inner self, and explore the true ideal of life art. I have tried to extend the path of "inspirational thinking" by continuing to explore the semiotics, symbols, and meanings of Eastern surrealist painting, in order to better understand spiritually-oriented art: 1. Image based cultural meaning and thinking splendor, 2. Meaning of self aware cultural signs and images, 3. Symbolic perceptive content and atmosphere, 4. Orientation of spiritual forms and the restoration of essence. I personally think, the so-called artistic way of Eastern ideals, should include be the coming together of subjective awareness, conscious temperament and nature. It is in this context that the artistic exploration of "Orient, Contemplation" is in accord with the Golden Mean, Eastern and Western flexibility, adaptability, and spiritual thinking systems. The creative perspective of "Ten Styles of the Literary Mind and Carving of Dragons" connects past and present as well as Chinese and Western styles. It is a convergence, like the restoration of spiritual energy. This is "virtual" thinking and practice, its purpose being to unveil the meaning behind subjective inner views and display "spiritually wise art" imbued with conscious freedom.

Outcome and direction of "Nature, togetherness"

From the interaction of artistic thinking and expressive forms, we can review important exhibition content and broadly know the artistic exploration and development direction of the artist. This clearly includes reflections on the origin of ink art water ink spirituality, the evolution of artistic spirituality and the stylistic expressionism of Eastern surrealism. Other than explaining the author's artistic development, it also elucidates the origin and transformation of the key styles while at the same time reflecting the spiritual ideal of "respecting one's own spirit." Basically, the author takes the natural application of subjective temperament, and imbues "art/reason" with artistic faith, showcasing experienced "emotions/ aesthetics" to reflect the evolutionary process of life existence. Moreover, as part of the pursuit of self actualization the thinking and reasoning of "quiet understanding," through the quiet introspection and reflection of "dedicated intellect," reveals the truth and reality of "dedicated knowledge." By following this spiritual concept, artistic thinking and creative practice, it is possible to offer a detailed clarification and illumination. It is hoped that the interplay of realism and surrealism will highlight the inspirational thinking of "reason/art."

The author believes that clarifying the thinking behind subjective awareness offers a subjective interpretation of true meaning. This unbiased spiritual awareness comes from the consistency of the "Doctrine of the Golden Mean." As such, the interplay of realist and surrealist thinking depends on us developing an objective understanding of vision integration. This interest in illusion is akin to the virtual spirit of "convergence," and thinking on "adaptability." Even the inspirational creation that originates in Revelation can be traced to experienced awareness of life. To some extent, this represents the "artistic aesthetics" of the Golden Mean, but it is even more the flexible application of "inspirational thinking" in a way that embraces both East and West.

Doctorate theses: "From Spiritual Vision, Illusion, and Subconsciousness"- exploring the signs, symbols, and meanings of surrealistic painting style in colored ink) (Taipei, National Taiwan Normal University Fine Art Research Institute literature)

Periodical article: Spiritual Thinking, Revitalized Reasoning - A Discussion on the Artistic View of Eastern Paintings from the Perspective of Modern Language) 45th Edition of (Claborate-style Painting Periodical) (Published by Taipei, ROC Claborate-style Painting Society)

專長類別	（1）美學史論研究：美學思想─藝術觀念─繪畫理論
	（2）藝術鑑賞講座：傳統研究─現代探索─當代實驗
	（3）專業諮詢顧問：鑑賞知識─投資理論─收藏實務
	（4）中西繪畫教學：國畫─水墨─書法─素描─水彩─油畫

藝術理念	（1）古今精神轉化・中西思想匯通	（7）關懷人文自然・省思文明現象
	（2）結合多元文化・創造民族特色	（8）綜觀天地造化・回歸性靈世界
	（3）反映生活現實・傳達時代見證	（9）主觀思維覺照・自我面目建構
	（4）根源生命體驗・呈現內在情思	（10）國際宏觀視野・地方本土情懷
	（5）理解藝術脈絡・顯示歷史真相	（11）超越事物表象・思索深層意義
	（6）感應現代氛圍・探索心理結構	（12）法理之外傳情・真善之內存美

李憶含

國立臺灣師範大學美術研究所　藝術學　博士

臺北　李憶含藝術工作室	主持教授
靈・上居 – 東方美學思想講堂	理論指導
東方藝術思想理論研究會	理論指導
中華美學史觀創作研究會	理論指導
臺北　國立國父紀念館生活美學班	水墨講師
慈濟大學　臺北社會教育推廣中心	書畫講師
臺北市　河洛漢詩學苑藝術研習班	書畫講師

學術經歷

國立臺灣師範大學美術研究所藝術學 博士	2006－2012
國立臺灣師範大學美術研究所創作組 碩士	1997－1999
國立臺灣師範大學美術學系 文學士	1979－1984
國立臺南藝術學院造形藝術研究所綜合評鑑合格	1983－1984

專業經歷

香港—海峽兩岸文化藝術交流協會	副秘書長
國立臺灣師範大學進修推廣部中西繪畫	講師
國立臺灣美術館美術研習班中西繪畫	講師
二十一世紀中國現代水墨畫會	理事
臺師大美研所一號窗畫會	副會長
中華民國元墨畫會	總幹事
臺北 師大藝術中心	主持教授
中華文化總會	會員
第三屆馬來西亞美術雙年展	評審委員
社團法人中華文化藝術創價協會	諮詢顧問
中華民族融合發展基金會	董事兼董事局主任秘書

重要策展

1989	現代仕女——夏之裸專題特展	（臺北・師大藝術中心）
1989	現代叢林——都市山水專題特展	（臺北・師大藝術中心）
1990	海峽掇英——神州與仙島專題特展	（臺北・師大藝術中心）

主要個展

1987　永遠的太魯——李憶含現代水墨畫展（臺北・華視藝術中心）

1989　月世界幻象——李憶含現代水墨畫展（臺中・臺中市立文化中心）

1993　臺灣・印象——李憶含現代水墨畫展（臺北・師大藝術中心）

1999　人文的關懷：思源・古風・映象——李憶含現代水墨畫展（臺北・臺師大美術系館）

2000　時代・映象——李憶含現代水墨畫展（臺北・國立臺灣藝術教育館）

　　　世紀新展望：自然・東方・本相——李憶含現代水墨畫展（臺南・永都藝術館、臺北・國父紀念館）

2002　萬象唯心經——李憶含現代水墨畫展（臺北・國父紀念館逸仙藝廊）

2003　東方・新象——李憶含現代水墨畫展（雲林・國立雲林科技大學藝術中心）

2004　繁華緣夢生——李憶含現代水墨畫展（臺北・國父紀念館逸仙藝廊）

2008　阿含經驗：現代荷——李憶含當代水墨創作展（臺北・國父紀念館逸仙藝廊）

2010　變異與歸元——李憶含當代水墨創作展（臺北・福華師大藝廊）

2012　靈視・幻象——李憶含當代水墨創作展（臺北・臺師大德群畫廊）

　　　靈視・幻象——李憶含當代水墨創作展（臺北・國父紀念館逸仙藝廊）

2014　彰文教化・八卦新氣——李憶含書法藝術創作展（彰化・八卦山大佛風景區臺灣文化創意中心）

2015　體時用中・觀象擬真——李憶含水墨藝術創作發表會（臺北・赫聲雲端會館）

　　　山海觀經・靈智顯——李憶含書法藝術創作展（臺北・蕙風堂書畫圖書）

　　　煙雨江南・風華延展——李憶含書法藝術師生作品展（臺北・文學叢林 - 紀州庵）

2017　東方・凝視——2017李憶含水墨藝術跨年特展（臺北・國父紀念館逸仙藝廊）

相關聯展

1981　中國美術協會聯展　作品〈山城月色〉（臺北・明生畫廊）

　　　全國青年書畫創作展　作品〈北城之秋〉（臺北・國父紀念館）

　　　全國青年書畫創作展　作品〈魚趣〉（基隆・基隆市立圖書館）

1982　臺灣全省美展　作品〈颱風前奏〉（臺北・臺灣省立博物館）

1983　光華青年寫生美展　作品〈臺北印象〉（臺北・國父紀念館）

1986　當代名家「吟秋」人物特展　作品〈秋思〉（臺北・華明藝廊）

　　　臺北教師美展　作品〈不歸鳥〉（臺北・臺北市立美術館）

　　　中華民國當代美展　作品〈雨荷〉（高雄・高雄市立文化中心）

1988　第五十一屆臺陽美術學會　作品〈塵緣〉、〈獨行〉（臺北・光復畫廊）

1989　中韓現代水墨聯展　作品〈幽岩覓趣〉（臺北・臺北市立美術館）

　　　當代名家畫馬特展　作品〈東風即景〉（臺北・國立臺灣藝術教育館）

　　　現代仕女——夏之裸　作品〈陰陽雙姝〉（臺北・師大藝術中心）

　　　現代叢林——都市山水專題特展　作品〈靈山對話〉（臺北・師大藝術中心）

　　　海峽掇英——神州與仙島專題特展　作品〈清岩記趣〉（臺北・師大藝術中心）

1990　現代水墨四人展　│作品〈古木秋蟬〉（臺北・師大藝術中心）

　　　　臺北市第十七界屆美展　│作品〈夜氣〉（臺北・臺北市立美術館）

　　　　美國五年巡迴展　│作品〈榴園記趣〉（美國・各大美術館）

1993　中韓水墨畫展　│作品〈中國風韻〉（臺北・中正藝廊）

1994　中韓水墨畫展　│作品〈懷古印象〉（韓國・漢城文藝振興院美術館）

1995　中韓水墨畫展　│作品〈夜氣〉（臺北・中正藝廊）

1996　中韓水墨畫展　│作品〈秋夜獨醒〉（韓國・漢城文藝振興院美術館）

1997　臺北－漢城－南京水墨畫聯展　│作品〈絕頂泰山〉（中國・江蘇省立美術館、臺北・國父紀念館）

1999　第十五屆全國美展　│作品〈思想蛻變〉（臺北・中正藝廊）

　　　　慈濟文化藝術獎學金作品聯展　│作品〈人文・自然〉等（花蓮・慈濟功德會主辦）

　　　　人文與藝術創作研究展　│作品〈蒸蒸日上〉（臺北・印儀學院、臺師大美研所共同主辦）

　　　　二十一世紀現代水墨畫聯展　│作品〈三月臺灣〉等（臺北・國父紀念館）

　　　　臺師大美研所一號窗畫會聯展　│作品〈自由心證〉等（臺南・永都藝術館）

2000　橘枳之變—東海大學與臺灣師大研究所水墨教學比較展　│作品〈古道夢迴〉等（臺中・臺中市文化中心、臺北・草土社）

　　　　師大美研所88級五人聯展　│作品〈天上人間〉等（臺北・臺北市立社教館）

　　　　臺師大美研所一號窗畫會聯展　│作品〈生生不息〉（高雄・名展藝術空間）

2001　第一道月光—蔡瑞月畫展　│作品〈新月之象〉等（臺北・鳳甲美術館）

　　　　中華民國第三屆現代水墨畫展　│作品〈古風新象〉等（臺北・中正藝廊）

　　　　10＋10＝21 臺北←→臺中展覽　│作品〈思想對話〉等（臺中・國立臺灣美術館）

　　　　第一屆愛我中華—中國畫油畫大展（中國・文化部中國群眾文化協會、臺灣・中華文化藝術基金會共同主辦）

2002　彩墨風華全國彩墨藝術大展　│作品〈千禧之夢〉等（臺中・臺中市文化局）

　　　　二十一世紀現代水墨聯展　│作品〈般若蜜多〉等（臺北・中正藝廊）

2003　國際彩墨布旗展　│作品〈東方勁紅〉等（臺中・臺中市文化局、法國、波蘭、美國、新加坡、馬來西亞巡迴展）

　　　　水墨新動向——二十一世紀現代水墨畫會聯展　│作品〈西藏之雲〉等（臺北・國父紀念館逸仙藝廊）

　　　　兩岸當代藝術家交流展　│作品〈世紀平安〉（臺中・臺中市文化局）

2004　水墨新動向——臺灣現代水墨畫展　│作品〈流動智慧〉等（中國・青島市文化博覽中心）

　　　　花樣臺北——一號窗畫會聯展　│作品〈青春蓮華〉等（臺北・天使美術館）

　　　　二十一世紀現代水墨畫會聯展　│作品〈世界屋脊〉等（臺中・逢甲大學藝術中心）

2005　水墨四重奏——曾肅良、黃智陽、呂坤和、李憶含書畫聯展　│作品〈文明省思〉等（臺北縣・臺北縣藝文中心藝文館）

2006　五嶽看山——海峽兩岸研究生五嶽文化考察寫生暨作品聯展　│作品〈千禧之夢〉等（北京・中央美術學院）

2007　慶祝中山樓建樓週年紀念「中山樓百景美展」　│作品〈風水陽明〉等（臺北・陽明山中山樓）

　　　　國父紀念館百美與吾土吾民聯展　│作品〈自有我在〉等（臺北・國父紀念館逸仙藝廊）

　　　　佛光山舉辦國際藝術獎「大慈大悲菩薩行——觀世音菩薩聖像畫展」　│作品〈自在蓮華〉（臺北・佛光緣美術館）

　　　　國際彩墨圖騰大展　│作品〈五行化生〉等（臺中・臺中市文化局）

　　　　立意出新——師大博士班聯展　│作品〈藍調夜曲〉等（臺北・法務部）

2008　中華兩岸美術學博士生創作交流展　│作品〈神思五岳〉等（臺北・國父紀念館逸仙藝廊）

2009　臺灣師範大學——韓國成均館大學師生交流展　│作品〈臺島安住〉等（臺北・師大畫廊）

　　　　兩岸當代名家畫油燈聯展　│〈蓮心光華〉（臺北・國父紀念館德明藝廊）

2010　國立臺灣師範大學美研所創作理論組博士班聯展　│作品〈青鳥始信〉等（臺北・國父紀念館逸仙藝廊）

　　　　中韓藝術交流展——臺灣師範大學 VS 韓國成均館大學　│作品〈幸運石云〉（臺北・國父紀念館逸仙書坊）

2011　新水墨的裂變——兩岸當代水墨創新展　作品〈曇花一現〉等（臺北・國父紀念館翠溪藝廊）

2012　龍行大運——兩岸精彩書畫名家聯展　作品〈五岳神思〉（臺北・國父紀念館德明藝廊）

　　　臺北釜山國際美術交流展　作品〈Mother・臺灣〉（韓國・釜山 / 美術城集團）

2013　程代勒、李憶含、喻幹當代水墨創作展　作品〈非思靈在〉等（美國・舊金山 / 中國畫廊）

　　　當代名家水墨書畫聯展　作品〈聲聲之喚〉等（美國・舊金山 / 中國畫廊）

　　　中華畫院藝術大展　作品〈三月臺灣〉（臺北・國父紀念館中山國家畫廊）

　　　兩岸情・心連心——中華兩岸書畫藝術交流展　作品〈三月臺灣〉（中國・北京 / 全國政協禮堂）

　　　弘藝敦誼、情繫中華——兩岸三地當代名家書畫展　作品〈思意幾何〉（美國・舊金山 / 硅谷亞洲藝術中心）

　　　法國羅浮宮卡魯塞爾藝術展獲選　作品〈天上人間〉（法國・巴黎 / 羅浮宮卡魯塞爾廳）

2014　美麗中國——海峽兩岸當代名人名家書畫巡展　作品〈千禧之夢〉（中國・江西 / 江西省美術館等）

　　　衍中華氣象・書兩岸同春——海峽兩岸知名書畫家作品聯展　作品〈夢迴東方〉等（中國・江蘇 / 蘇州太湖大學堂）

　　　新東方現代書畫協會作品聯展　作品〈三月臺灣〉等（基隆・基隆市文化局一樓藝廊）

　　　第二屆臺灣書畫百人大展　作品〈遠芳春意〉（臺北・國立中正紀念堂中正藝廊）

　　　中華情・心連心——海峽兩岸書畫藝術交流展　作品〈魚說那島〉等（中國・山東 / 濰坊齊魯臺灣城）

　　　海峽兩岸情——臺灣書畫名家交流展　作品〈魚說那島〉等（中國・江西 / 江西省美術館）

　　　中華兩岸藝術名家創作展　作品〈歡・101〉等（臺北・臺北大樓中華藝術館）

2016　中國夢・絲路情——兩岸書畫名家作品（陝西）邀請展　作品〈敦煌風月〉等（中國・陝西省美術館）

　　　第三屆臺灣書畫百人大展　作品〈呼喚東方〉（臺北・國立中正紀念堂中正藝廊）

2017　臺灣十名家中國畫安徽滁州文化交流聯展　作品〈文心雕龍・十式〉（中國・安徽 / 滁州美術館）

　　　戲韻藝情——戲曲人物國際書畫名家邀請展　作品〈遠芳春意〉（臺北・國立國父紀念館文華軒）

　　　海峽兩岸文藝界迎春畫展　作品〈Mother・臺灣〉（臺北・臺北市議會）

　　　第一屆香港「全球水墨畫大展」　作品〈人文・自然〉（香港・香港會議展覽中心）

2018　第一屆傳統新韻——當代名家美展　作品〈春秋鳥來〉等（臺北・國父紀念館博愛藝廊）

　　　水墨加一臺——臺灣當代名家國畫展　作品〈太素元清 - 極精義〉等（溫哥華・國際畫廊）

義賣活動

1993　十五年阿桂與畫家的溫馨接送情畫展　作品〈夜夜如此〉等（臺北・東之畫廊）

2009　師大教授及校友義賣聯展　作品〈赫然當陽〉等（臺北縣・新莊藝文中心）

2009　藝術義賣——愛心賑災展覽　作品〈相思千里〉等（中華民國紅十字總會等、臺北・國立國父紀念館）

2009　扇撥文化善撥愛——2009臺灣百扇名人錄畫展　作品〈五四運動〉等（中華倫理教育學會等、臺北・國立國父紀念館）

2018　應邀參加北教大人文藝術季——「抽詩剝繭—向陽原創詩集音樂會」，現場書寫　作品〈行旅〉（巨作4x16尺）（臺北教育大學、臺北・創意館雨賢廳）

獎勵摘要

2001　榮獲第一屆愛我中華——中國畫油畫大展優秀獎
　　　（中國・文化部——中國群眾文化協會、臺灣・中華文化藝術基金會等 共同主辦。）

2007　榮獲佛光山舉辦國際藝術獎「大慈大悲菩薩行──觀世音菩薩聖像畫展」第一名（臺北・佛光緣美術館主辦）

2009　榮獲中華文化傳播貢獻獎（世界華人精英雜誌社・世界漢學出版及中文傳媒協會 主辦）

2017　獲聘2017第十二屆全球城市形象大使暨全球城市小姐（先生）選拔大賽藝術顧問。

　　　獲聘臺北嘎檔巴文化節──中華書畫大展暨高峰論壇共同策劃人與講座主持。

作品曾獲中日文化交流展、中部五縣市寫生展、光華國際寫生展佳作與臺北市十七界屆美展優選，並獲選各項全國美展、全國青年創作獎、全省美展和臺北縣、市美展，以及南瀛美展、臺陽美展等等）

專訪報導

1989　漢聲廣播電臺專訪報導，介紹〈永遠的太魯〉展覽之精神理念，概述文人思想、風格內容與傳統研究。

1993　警察廣播電臺專訪報導，介紹〈月世界幻象〉展覽之藝術思想，概述美學內涵、形式表現與現代探索。

1994　*Unique Artistry* 雜誌專訪報導，介紹〈空靈寫意的國畫藝術〉，概述藝術特徵、技法表現與前衛實驗。

1999　《中國時報》、《民生報》、《聯合報》、《中時晚報》與《大成報》專文報導，介紹〈人文的關懷──思源・古風・映象〉，概述東西遇合、高度思想與精神會通。

2008　《大紀元》新聞彭秋燕專訪報導，介紹〈西洋情人節─李憶含談美麗的藝術〉，概述精神理念、藝術思想與創作實踐。

2009　《經濟日報》唐煒哲專訪報導，介紹〈東方新象──探索人文的創作者〉，概述主體自覺、情思美感與精神意趣。

2013　達威光臨傳播媒體專訪報導，介紹〈天曉樓──陳丹誠書畫藝術〉，概述中國意向、美學特質與觀念轉化。

2014　都會週刊時報《多汁報》專訪報導，介紹〈李憶含書畫形神兩全──創作龍玉詩夢靈佳構〉，概述東方思惟、藝術圖式與風格型態。

　　　《PEOPLE 民眾網》專訪報導，介紹〈彰文教化・八卦新氣──2014 李憶含書法藝術創作展〉，概述當代表現、創作主軸與思想理路。

　　　北京中央電視書畫頻道「美術新聞」，介紹〈彰文教化・八卦新氣──2014李憶含書法藝術創作展〉，概述東方文人、嚴肅思考與精神自覺。

　　　臺灣媒體《赫聲現場》新聞專訪報導，介紹〈彰文教化・八卦新氣──2014李憶含書法藝術創作展〉，概述靈智雙關、美藝契合與活性創造。

2018　北京《台聲》（*TAISHENG*）雜誌社兩岸藝文專題，介紹曾長生〈李憶含的靈動水墨思維演化〉（北京・《台聲》雜誌社）

　　　北京《台聲》（*TAISHENG*）雜誌社兩岸藝文專題，介紹李憶含「靈思百度・活化理路──從當代語境談東方繪畫藝術觀」（北京・《台聲》雜誌社）

　　　北京《台聲》（*TAISHENG*）雜誌社兩岸藝文專題，介紹李憶含「從『藝道美學・靈動思惟』─探討 體『時』用『中』的思考與實踐」（北京・《台聲》雜誌社）

藝評撰述

1999　臺灣師範大學王友俊教授撰文評述，介紹〈人文的關懷──思源、古風、映象〉，概述有關精神理念與風格意趣。

　　　臺灣師範大學梁秀中教授撰文評述，介紹〈心象為上・創意表現──談李憶含的藝術取向〉，概述有關藝術思想與圖式面貌。

　　　臺灣師範大學王哲雄教授撰文評述，介紹〈李憶含貫串古今兼顧中西的多元文化創作觀〉，概述有關創作實踐與技法表現。

　　　臺灣師範大學羅芳教授撰文評述，介紹〈茁壯成長──談李憶含〉，概述有關文化意涵與精神自覺。

　　　臺灣師範大學袁金塔教授撰文評述，介紹〈東方新象・臺灣本色──談李憶含的水墨創作〉，概述有關歷史演變與思想理路。

2002　臺灣師範大學曾肅良教授撰文評述，介紹〈夢的光譜──讀李憶含「繁華緣夢生」系列作品〉，概述有關哲學探微與東方典型。

2011　新水墨的裂變──兩岸當代水墨創新展　作品〈曇花一現〉等（臺北‧國父紀念館翠溪藝廊）

2012　龍行大運──兩岸精彩書畫名家聯展　作品〈五岳神思〉（臺北‧國父紀念館德明藝廊）

　　　臺北釜山國際美術交流展　作品〈Mother‧臺灣〉（韓國‧釜山／美術城集團）

2013　程代勒、李憶含、喻幹當代水墨創作展　作品〈非思靈在〉等（美國‧舊金山／中國畫廊）

　　　當代名家水墨書畫聯展　作品〈聲聲之喚〉等（美國‧舊金山／中國畫廊）

　　　中華畫院藝術大展　作品〈三月臺灣〉（臺北‧國父紀念館中山國家畫廊）

　　　兩岸情‧心連心──中華兩岸書畫藝術交流展　作品〈三月臺灣〉（中國‧北京／全國政協禮堂）

　　　弘藝敦誼、情繫中華──兩岸三地當代名家書畫展　作品〈思意幾何〉（美國‧舊金山／硅谷亞洲藝術中心）

　　　法國羅浮宮卡魯塞爾藝術展獲選　作品〈天上人間〉（法國‧巴黎／羅浮宮卡魯塞爾廳）

2014　美麗中國──海峽兩岸當代名人名家書畫巡展　作品〈千禧之夢〉（中國‧江西／江西省美術館等）

　　　衍中華氣象‧書兩岸同春──海峽兩岸知名書畫家作品聯展　作品〈夢迴東方〉等（中國‧江蘇／蘇州太湖大學堂）

　　　新東方現代書畫協會作品聯展　作品〈三月臺灣〉等（基隆‧基隆市文化局一樓藝廊）

　　　第二屆臺灣書畫百人大展　作品〈遠芳春意〉（臺北‧國立中正紀念堂中正藝廊）

　　　中華情‧心連心──海峽兩岸書畫藝術交流展　作品〈魚說那島〉等（中國‧山東／濰坊齊魯臺灣城）

　　　海峽兩岸情──臺灣書畫名家交流展　作品〈魚說那島〉等（中國‧江西／江西省美術館）

　　　中華兩岸藝術名家創作展　作品〈歡‧101〉等（臺北‧臺北大樓中華藝術館）

2016　中國夢‧絲路情──兩岸書畫名家作品（陝西）邀請展　作品〈敦煌風月〉等（中國‧陝西省美術館）

　　　第三屆臺灣書畫百人大展　作品〈呼喚東方〉（臺北‧國立中正紀念堂中正藝廊）

2017　臺灣十名家中國畫安徽滁州文化交流聯展　作品〈文心雕龍‧十式〉（中國‧安徽／滁州美術館）

　　　戲韻藝情──戲曲人物國際書畫名家邀請展　作品〈遠芳春意〉（臺北‧國立國父紀念館文華軒）

　　　海峽兩岸文藝界迎春畫展　作品〈Mother‧臺灣〉（臺北‧臺北市議會）

　　　第一屆香港「全球水墨畫大展」　作品〈人文‧自然〉（香港‧香港會議展覽中心）

2018　第一屆傳統新韻──當代名家美展　作品〈春秋烏來〉等（臺北‧國父紀念館博愛藝廊）

　　　水墨加一臺──臺灣當代名家國畫展　作品〈太素元清 - 極精義〉等（溫哥華‧國際畫廊）

義賣活動

1993　十五年阿桂與畫家的溫馨接送情畫展　作品〈夜夜如此〉等（臺北‧東之畫廊）

2009　師大教授及校友義賣聯展　作品〈赫然當陽〉等（臺北縣‧新莊藝文中心）

2009　藝術義賣──愛心賑災展覽　作品〈相思千里〉等（中華民國紅十字總會等、臺北‧國立國父紀念館）

2009　扇撥文化善撥愛──2009臺灣百扇名人錄畫展　作品〈五四運動〉等（中華倫理教育學會等、臺北‧國立國父紀念館）

2018　應邀參加北教大人文藝術季──「抽詩剝蘭─向陽原創詩集音樂會」，現場書寫　作品〈行旅〉（巨作4x16尺）（臺北教育大學、臺北‧創意館雨賢廳）

獎勵摘要

2001　榮獲第一屆愛我中華──中國畫油畫大展優秀獎
　　　（中國‧文化部──中國群眾文化協會、臺灣‧中華文化藝術基金會等 共同主辦。）

2007   榮獲佛光山舉辦國際藝術獎「大慈大悲菩薩行——觀世音菩薩聖像畫展」第一名（臺北・佛光緣美術館主辦）
2009   榮獲中華文化傳播貢獻獎（世界華人精英雜誌社・世界漢學出版及中文傳媒協會 主辦）
2017   獲聘2017第十二屆全球城市形象大使暨全球城市小姐（先生）選拔大賽藝術顧問。
        獲聘臺北嘎檔巴文化節——中華書畫大展暨高峰論壇共同策劃人與講座主持。

作品曾獲中日文化交流展、中部五縣市寫生展、光華國際寫生展佳作與臺北市十七界屆美展優選，並獲選各項全國美展、全國青年創作獎、全省美展和臺北縣、市美展，以及南瀛美展、臺陽美展等等）

專訪報導

1989   漢聲廣播電臺專訪報導，介紹〈永遠的太魯〉展覽之精神理念，概述文人思想、風格內容與傳統研究。
1993   警察廣播電臺專訪報導，介紹〈月世界幻象〉展覽之藝術思想，概述美學內涵、形式表現與現代探索。
1994   *Unique Artistry* 雜誌專訪報導，介紹〈空靈寫意的國畫藝術〉，概述藝術特徵、技法表現與前衛實驗。
1999   《中國時報》、《民生報》、《聯合報》、《中時晚報》與《大成報》專文報導，介紹〈人文的關懷——思源・古風・映象〉，概述東西遇合、高度思想與精神會通。
2008   《大紀元》新聞彭秋燕專訪報導，介紹〈西洋情人節—李憶含談美麗的藝術〉，概述精神理念、藝術思想與創作實踐。
2009   《經濟日報》唐煒哲專訪報導，介紹〈東方新象——探索人文的創作者〉，概述主體自覺、情思美感與精神意趣。
2013   達威光臨傳播媒體專訪報導，介紹〈天曉樓——陳丹誠書畫藝術〉，概述中國意向、美學特質與觀念轉化。
2014   都會週刊時報《多汁報》專訪報導，介紹〈李憶含書畫形神兩全——創作龍玉詩夢靈佳構〉，概述東方思惟、藝術圖式與風格型態。
        《PEOPLE 民眾網》專訪報導，介紹〈彰文教化・八卦新氣——2014 李憶含書法藝術創作展〉，概述當代表現、創作主軸與思想理路。
        北京中央電視書畫頻道「美術新聞」，介紹〈彰文教化・八卦新氣——2014李憶含書法藝術創作展〉，概述東方文人、嚴肅思考與精神自覺。
        臺灣媒體《赫聲現場》新聞專訪報導，介紹〈彰文教化・八卦新氣——2014李憶含書法藝術創作展〉，概述靈智雙關、美藝契合與活性創造。
2018   北京《台聲》（*TAISHENG*）雜誌社兩岸藝文專題，介紹曾長生〈李憶含的靈動水墨思維演化〉（北京・《台聲》雜誌社）
        北京《台聲》（*TAISHENG*）雜誌社兩岸藝文專題，介紹李憶含「靈思百度・活化理路——從當代語境談東方繪畫藝術觀」（北京・《台聲》雜誌社）
        北京《台聲》（*TAISHENG*）雜誌社兩岸藝文專題，介紹李憶含「從『藝道美學・靈動思惟』—探討 體『時』用『中』的思考與實踐」（北京・《台聲》雜誌社）

藝評撰述

1999   臺灣師範大學王友俊教授撰文評述，介紹〈人文的關懷——思源、古風、映象〉，概述有關精神理念與風格意趣。
        臺灣師範大學梁秀中教授撰文評述，介紹〈心象為上・創意表現——談李憶含的藝術取向〉，概述有關藝術思想與圖式面貌。
        臺灣師範大學王哲雄教授撰文評述，介紹〈李憶含貫串古今兼顧中西的多元文化創作觀〉，概述有關創作實踐與技法表現。
        臺灣師範大學羅芳教授撰文評述，介紹〈茁壯成長——談李憶含〉，概述有關文化意涵與精神自覺。
        臺灣師範大學袁金塔教授撰文評述，介紹〈東方新象・臺灣本色——談李憶含的水墨創作〉，概述有關歷史演變與思想理路。
2002   臺灣師範大學曾肅良教授撰文評述，介紹〈夢的光譜——讀李憶含「繁華緣夢生」系列作品〉，概述有關哲學探微與東方典型。

2004 臺灣師範大學曾肅良教授撰文評述，介紹〈水月空花，萬象唯心——評析李憶含「萬象唯心經」彩墨展〉，概述有關美學內涵與藝術特徵。

2018 雄獅美術黃長春撰文評述，介紹〈東方・凝視——李憶含〉〈臺北・《人間福報》〉，概述有關藝道美學與靈動思惟。

臺灣藝術大學曾長生教授撰文評述，介紹〈「李憶含的靈動水墨思維演化」〉，概述有關變通會適與唯易思想。

刊載記錄

1994 登錄《臺藝藝術家名人錄》 作品〈靜觀自得〉（臺北・藝術家出版社）

1996 登錄《中國美術書法界名人名作博覽》 作品〈時空印象〉（中國・中國國際廣播出版社）

2011 登錄莊坤良著《流離（Traveling Aesthetics）—— 藝術英文散集》 作品〈千里江行〉等（臺北・文鶴出版社）

2014 登錄中國・北京《藝術沙龍（Art Sason）—— 臺灣博士畫家新探索》 作品〈曇花一現〉等（中國・人民美術出版社）

專題講座

2008 樹林市公所舉辦藝文類專題講座，主講：「西洋情人節——談美麗的藝術」（臺北・樹林三多圖書館）

2013 天籟吟社舉辦古典詩詞專題講座，主講：「從『靈』活『運』用——談詩情與畫意的互通性」（臺北・臺北天籟吟社）

2014 臺北西南區扶輪社藝術專題講座，主講：「淺談——藝術鑑賞、投資與收藏」（臺北・臺北西南區扶輪社）

2015 臺北南天區扶輪社藝術專題講座，主講：「淺談——藝術鑑賞、投資與收藏」（臺北・臺北南天區扶輪社）

2016 臺北西南區扶輪社藝術專題講座，主講：「智者品味——自然、人生與藝術」（臺北・臺北西南區扶輪社）

2017 兩岸書畫名家交流展——海峽書畫藝術論談，主講：「靈智演藝——水墨美學與東方精神（臺北・張榮發基金會藝術展覽館）

臺北嘎檔巴文化節——中華書畫大展暨高峰論壇，主講：「藝道美學——東方精神與水墨復興」（臺北・張榮發基金會藝術展覽館）

臺北嘎檔巴文化節——中華書畫大展暨高峰論壇，主講：「東方凝視——書道美學與靈智演藝」（臺北・張榮發基金會藝術展覽館）

「東方・凝視」系列專題講座，主講：「淺談——中華美學應運而生」（臺北・潘氏會館）

2018 「東方・凝視」系列專題講座，主講：「淺談——東方文化價值走向」（臺北・潘氏會館）

「東方・凝視」系列專題講座，主講：「淺談——東方文化與藝術精神」（臺北・法吉歐利音樂廳）

「東方・凝視」系列專題講座，主講：「淺談——東方文化與水墨美學」（臺北・逸昇設計瘋紙文創）

「東方・凝視」系列專題講座，主講：「淺談——東方文化的藝術美學」（臺北・臺北 黎畫廊）

「東方・凝視」系列專題講座，主講：「淺談——東方文化與書道美學」（臺北・松山文創園區）

「東方・凝視」系列專題講座，主講：「淺談——東西藝術的美學內涵」（臺北・美商惠而適臺灣分公司）

「東方・凝視」系列專題講座，主講：「淺談——東方藝術的精神品格」（臺北・全國社團領袖總會）

臺北淡江大學藝術鑑賞專題講座，主講：「淺談——現代書法藝術的發展」（臺北・淡江大學鍾靈化學館）

臺北銘傳大學藝術鑑賞專題講座，主講：「淺談——東靈西實的藝術美學」（臺北・銘傳大學城區部）

2018上海馳翰拍藝術賣公司專題講座，主講：「淺談——藝術鑑賞、投資與收藏」（臺北・上海馳翰臺北辦事處）

2018馬來西亞第一藝術空間專題講座，主講：「淺談——藝術鑑賞、投資與收藏」（馬來西亞・第一藝術空間）

頒獎活動

2013 應邀擔任第四屆金赫獎全球藝術大賽（書法類別 - 社會大專組）頒獎人（社團法人臺灣文創媒體藝術推廣協會等 主辦）

2015 應邀擔任第五屆金赫獎全球藝術大賽（水墨類別 - 社會大專組）頒獎人（社團法人臺灣文創媒體藝術推廣協會等 主辦）

出席會議

1997　黃君璧教授百年誕辰紀念國際學術研討會（國立臺灣師範大學美術系主辦）

1998　21世紀視覺藝術新展望國際學術研討會（國立臺灣師範大學美術學系主辦）

1999　五十年來臺灣美術教育學術研討會（國立臺灣師範大學美術學系主辦）

2002　水墨畫理論與創作國際學術研討會（國立臺灣師範大學美術學系主辦）

2006　海峽兩岸研究生五嶽文化考察寫生暨作品聯展研討會（北京・中央美術學院主辦）

2007　海峽兩岸研究生五嶽文化考察寫生暨作品聯展研討會（北京・中央美術學院主辦）

2008　緣筆墨之外──中國書法史跨領域國際學術研討會（臺北・國立臺灣師範大學美術學系主辦）

　　　新象──2009兩岸當代水墨展座談會（臺中・國立臺灣美術館主辦）

　　　音緣──當代書畫家相約在宜蘭談書畫藝術座談會（宜蘭・佛光山蘭陽別院國際會議廳）

2009　世界華人著名美術家環球和平之旅訪臺展覽會（臺北・臺北市政府會議室）

　　　中原文化寶島行──文化高峰論壇（臺北・國賓大飯店會議廳）

2010　大道同行──兩岸中國畫藝術展暨學術研討會（臺北・國父紀念館逸仙藝廊）

2012　匯墨高升──國際水墨大展暨學術研討會（臺北・國立臺灣師範大學美術學系主辦）

2013　中華畫院藝術大展暨學術研討會（臺北・國父紀念館中山講堂）

　　　覃志剛《鎔鑄丹青》／海峽兩岸藝術家座談會（臺北・國立臺灣師範大學主辦）

2014　國立國父紀念館「國父銅像揭幕儀式」（臺北・國父紀念館史蹟東室）

　　　第四屆當代中國畫學術論壇（臺北・國立臺灣師範大學美術學系主辦）

　　　參加「革命・復興──劉國松繪畫大展」研討會（臺北・國立臺灣師範大學美術學系主辦）

2018　參加「2018第二屆兩岸人文名家論壇理事會啟航儀式」（臺北・圓山大飯店國際會議廳）

學術著作

1987　《中國水墨系列──山水祕訣》（臺北・北星圖書公司出版）

1989　《素描精要解析》（臺中・國立臺灣美術館出版）

1990　《高工職美術課本》（臺北・儒林圖書公司出版）

1999　《人文的關懷──思源・古風・映象》碩士論文（臺北・國立臺灣師範大學美術研究所文獻）

2000　《東方新象──李憶含作品集》（臺北・中國風藝術研究會出版）

2002　《萬象唯心經──李憶含現代水墨藝術》（臺北・中國風藝術研究會出版）

2012　《從「靈視、幻象與潛意識流」──探討彩墨超現實畫風的符號、象徵與意涵》博士論文（臺北・國立臺灣師範大學美術研究所文獻）

發表文章

2008　〈從變異與歸元─談水墨精神的超現實性〉於《視覺藝術論壇》第5期（嘉義・國立嘉義大學人文藝術學院美術學系／視覺藝術研究所）

2014　〈「靈思百度・活化理路」──從當代語境談東方繪畫藝術觀〉於《工筆畫期刊》第45期（臺北・中華民國工筆畫學會）

2015　〈從「立象與盡意」──談東方藝術的精神／表現說〉（一）於《孔學與人生》第72期（臺北・中國孔學會）

2016　〈從「立象與盡意」──談東方藝術的精神／表現說〉（二）於《工筆畫期刊》第50期（臺北・中華民國工筆畫學會）

2017　〈從「立象與盡意」──談東方藝術的精神／表現說〉（三）於《藝響》第12期（臺北・中華全球文創協會）

旅遊寫生

曾至韓國、泰國、印尼、澳洲、紐西蘭、新加坡、馬來西亞、菲律賓、加拿大等國參觀研究,並在中國大陸山東、山西、河南、河北、浙江、四川、湖南、湖北、江蘇、安徽、江西、福建、廣東、廣西、雲南、貴州、陝西、甘肅、寧夏、青海、新疆與西藏等地旅遊寫生,且於2007年與2008年,參加五嶽看山-海峽兩岸研究生文化考察暨寫生活動,在五嶽(泰山、華山、衡山、恒山、嵩山)形象中得到激、觸、感、發,於人文景觀裡獲致形、神、理、趣。此外,也到山東青島博物館、北京中央美術學院、上海當代藝術博物館、蘇州博術館、甘肅蘭州大學和廣州炎黃美術館等處探索學習,以期蒐集東西方的藝術型態及特色,包括有關傳統美學風格與理念、現代藝術形式和題材,乃至當代創作技法及資料。

其他事宜

應邀慈濟文化藝術拍賣鑑識諮詢、參加佛光山舉辦教師研習營、為國際扶輪社南海分會做藝術賞析;於慶祝中山樓建樓40週年紀念時,協助籌備「中山樓百景美展」;為臺灣師範大學美研所創作理論組博士班聯展,專文撰稿介紹展覽特色與風格型態。曾經主辦中西融合的藝術教學,具有三十三年理論與實務經驗,並且成立藝術經紀之專業畫廊;同時擔任公私立學校寫生美展指導、文化基金會繪畫比賽評審,以及中國青年救國團西畫班講師、臺北市河洛漢詩學苑書法班講師。此外,接受民間企業與相關單位委託,擔任藝術研究、諮詢和鑑定顧問,提供有關作品投資、收藏及拍賣知識。

Lee Yi-han
Graduate Institute of Fine Arts, National Taiwan Normal University, Doctor of Fine Arts

Lee Yi-Han Art Studio, Taipei	Managing Professor
Elite Spirituality Dwelling- Eastern Aesthetic Philosophy Forum	Dissertation Guidance
Eastern Art Philosophical Theory Research Association	Dissertation Guidance
History of Chinese Aesthetics Research Association	Dissertation Guidance
National Dr. Sun Yat-sen Memorial Hall Lifestyle Aesthetics Class, Taipei	Ink Painting Lecturer
Continuing Education Center of Tzu Chi University, Taipei	Calligraphy and Painting Lecturer
Art Class of Hoklo Han Poetry Academy, Taipei	Calligraphy Lecturer

Education

2006-2012   Graduate Institute of Fine Arts, National Taiwan Normal University, Doctor of Fine Arts

1997-1999   Graduate Institute of Fine Arts, National Taiwan Normal University, Master of Fine Arts (Art Creation)

1979-1984   Department of Fine Arts, National Taiwan Normal University, Bachelor of Fine Arts

1983-1984   Graduate Institute of Plastic Arts - Tainan National University of the Arts Comprehensive Evaluation Qualification

Professional Experience

Hong Kong-Cross Straits Cultural and Art Exchange Association	Deputy Secretary-General
School of Continuing Education, National Taiwan Normal University	Chinese and Western Painting Lecturer
Art Class at the National Taiwan Museum of Fine Arts	Chinese and Western Painting Lecturer
21th Century Chinese Modern Ink Painting Association	Board Member
No. 1 Window Painting Society, Graduate Institute of Fine Arts, National Taiwan Normal University	Deputy Director
Yuanmo Painting Society	Executive Secretary
Art Center of National Taiwan Normal University (NTNU), Taipei	Managing Professor
The 3rd Malaysia Biennale Art Exhibition	Judge
Taiwan Soka Association	Adviser
Chinese People's Integrated Development Foundation	Chairman and Board of Directors Chief Secretary

Select Curatorial Work

1989   Modern Ladies – Summer Nudity Feature Exhibition, Art Center of National Taiwan Normal University, Taipei

1989   Modern Jungle – Urban Landscape Feature Exhibition, Art Center of National Taiwan Normal University, Taipei

1990   Selecting the Finest Blossoms Across the Strait - Divine Land and Celestial Island Feature Exhibition, Art Center of National Taiwan Normal University, Taipei

Select Solo Exhibitions

1987   Eternal Tai Lu – Lee Yi-Han Modern Ink Painting Exhibition, CTV Art Center, Taipei

1989   Moon World Illusion - Lee Yi-Han Modern Ink Painting Exhibition, Taichung City Cultural Center, Taichung

1993   Taiwan - image - Lee Yi-Han Modern Ink Painting Exhibition, Art Center of NTNU, Taipei

1999   Humanistic Compassion: Origin, Antiquity, Impression - Lee Yi-Han Modern Ink Painting Exhibition, Department of Fine Arts, NTNU, Taipei

2000   Epoch, Impression- Lee Yi-Han Modern Ink Painting Exhibition, National Taiwan Arts Education Center, Taipei

2000   New Century Prospects: Nature, East, Current State- Lee Yi-Han Modern Ink Painting Exhibition,
        Yung Tu Museum of Art, Tainan; National Dr. Sun Yat-sen Memorial Hall, Taipei

2002   Vientiane Heart Sutra - Lee Yi-Han Modern Ink Painting Exhibition,
        Yat-sen Gallery, National Dr. Sun Yat-sen Memorial Hall, Taipei

2003   East/ New Image - Lee Yi-Han Modern Ink Painting Exhibition,
        Art Center, National Yunlin University of Science and Technology, Yunlin

2004   Prosperous Destiny and Dream, Life- Lee Yi-Han Modern Ink Painting Exhibition,
        Yat-sen Gallery, National Dr. Sun Yat-sen Memorial Hall, Taipei

2008   Agama Experience: Modern Lotus - Lee Yi-Han Contemporary Ink Painting Exhibition,
        Yat-sen Gallery, National Dr. Sun Yat-sen Memorial Hall, Taipei

2010   Variation and Back-To-The-Origin- Lee Yi-Han Contemporary Ink Painting Exhibition, Howard NTNU Salon, Taipei

2012   Spiritual Vision, Illusion - Lee Yi-Han Contemporary Ink Painting Exhibition, Teh-Chun Art Gallery, Taipei

        Spiritual Vision, Illusion - Lee Yi-Han Contemporary Ink Painting Exhibition,
        Yat-sen Gallery, National Dr. Sun Yat-sen Memorial Hall, Taipei

2014   Changhua Education and Culture, New Energy in Bagua- Lee Yi-Han Calligraphy Art Exhibition,
        Taiwan Cultural and Creative Center, Mt. Bagua Scenic Area, Changhua

2015   Thinking and Practice in Using the Doctrine of the Golden Mean to Experience Change
        - Lee Yi-Han Ink Painting Exhibition, He Sheng Cloud Salon, Taipei

        Seeing Classic of Mountains and Seas, Manifestation of Spirituality and Wisdom-
        Lee Yi-Han Calligraphy Art Exhibition, Hui Feng Tang, Taipei

        Misty River South, Extending Splendor-Lee Yi-Han Calligraphy Art Teacher-Student Joint Exhibition,
        Kishu An Forest of Literature, Taipei

2017   Orient, Contemplation - 2017 Special New Year Countdown Exhibition for Li Yi-Han Water Ink Arts,
        Yat-sen Gallery, National Dr. Sun Yat-sen Memorial Hall, Taipei

Academic Publications

1987   "Chinese Ink Painting Series – Tips on Landscape", North Star Books, Taipei

1989   "Essential Analysis on Sketching", National Taiwan Museum of Fine Arts, Taichung

1990   "High SchoolArt Textbook", Scholars Books, Taipei

1999   "Humanistic Compassion: Origin, Antiquity, Impression", master's thesis,
        Archive of the Graduate Institute of Fine Arts, National Taiwan Normal University

2000   "East/ New Image – Work Collection of Lee Yi-Han", Chinoiserie Art Research Association, Taipei

2002   "Vientiane Heart Sutra - Lee Yi-Han Modern Ink Painting Exhibition", Chinoiserie Art Research Association, Taipei

2012   Doctorate theses: "From Spiritual Vision, Illusion, and Subconsciousness"- exploring the signs, symbols, and meanings
        of surrealistic painting style in colored ink, Archive of the Graduate Institute of Fine Arts, National Taiwan Normal University

Published Essays

2008   "Discussing the Surrealism of Ink Spirit - From the Perspective of Variation and Back-
        To-The-Origin", *Visual Arts Forum*, 5th issue, (Department of Fine Arts & Graduate Institute
        of Visual Arts of theCollege of Humanities and Arts, National Chiayi University, Chiayi)

2014   "Vast and Flexible Ideas, Invigorated Ways of Thinking – On Eastern Painting's Art Perspective
        Using ContemporaryRhetoric", *Gongbi Periodical*, 45th issue (Gonbi Society of ROC, Taipei)

2015   "Discussing the Ethos/Expressions of Eastern Artfrom 'Established Figures to Completely
        Express Meanings'" (I),*Confucianism and Humanity*, 72nd issue (China Confucius Society, Taipei)

2016   "Discussing the Ethos/Expressions of Eastern Art from 'Established Figures to Completely
        Express Meanings'"(II), *Gongbi Periodical*, 50th issue (Gonbi Society of ROC, Taipei)

2017   "Discussing the Ethos/Expressions of Eastern Art from 'Established Figures to Completely
        Express Meanings'" (III), *Art Resonance*, 12th issue
        (Chinese Global Cultural and Creative Association, Taipei)

生活留眞 —

001

009

004

005

003

002

010

006

007

008

個人選照

001　前往臺北旅遊局於新聞發布現場留影。
002　中華兩岸藝術名家創作展於會場留影。
003　五嶽看山活動時於北京中央美院留影。
004　江南行旅藝術采風於蘇州博物館留影。
005　海峽兩岸交流活動於北京臺灣館留影。

006　參加中華文化總會舉辦藝文聯誼茶會。
007　參加臺北佛光山慈善活動於展場留影。
008　參觀北京中央電視臺於壹號塔樓留影。
009　參觀展覽時於何創時書法基金會留影。
010　黔山秀水行旅於貴陽諾富特酒店留影。

文化考察

001 中華文化總會第七屆第一次會員大會。	007 參訪敦煌藝術研究所時應邀現場揮毫。
002 五嶽看山活動時，於中央美術學院合影。	008 參觀江蘇鎮江博物館展覽時現場留影。
003 五嶽看山活動開幕典禮時，潘公愷致詞。	009 參觀吳冠中畫展於中華藝術宮內留影。
004 臺灣十名家中國畫聯展時遊豐樂亭。	010 與江明賢、薛永年、孫景波教授合影。
005 於上海奧運「中華藝術宮」現場留影。	011 與范光陵等倡導東方文藝復興時合影。
006 於香港─海峽兩岸文化藝術交流協會。	

藝術交流

001 前往參觀黃光男教授展覽時於現場留影。
002 於春茗酒會與陸委會副主委劉德勳合影。
003 於展場與王建煊院長、趙昌平委員合影。
004 參觀展覽時，和臺灣知名教授現場留影。
005 參觀展覽時，和知名主持人於現場留影。
006 參觀展覽時，和高行健教授於現場留影。
007 於北京第三屆海峽兩岸電視藝術節留影。
008 於畫會聯展與郭文夫教授等人宴席合影。

009 全國水墨畫大展時與劉國松教授合影。
010 與中央美術學院羅世平教授臺北合影。
011 與前中國時報發行人林聖芬等人合影。
012 與江明賢教授於中嶽嵩山考察時留影。
013 應邀前往人文遠雄博物館參觀時留影。
014 應邀前往山東濰坊藝術交流現場留影。
015 應邀參加長流美術館年度的慶祝晚會。

教學推廣

001 戶外教學時於臺大農場現場寫生合影。	007 於國立臺灣師範大學進修推廣部教學。
002 臺北東區的藝術基地一李憶含工作室。	008 前往中山堂臺北書院現場示範時留影。
003 臺北國父紀念館東方水墨理論與創作。	009 參訪昔日教學所在一國立臺灣美術館。
004 臺北國父紀念館畫展時專題講座現場。	010 參觀臺灣師範大學研究所畢業作品展。
005 臺北慈濟大學社會推廣部書畫班教學。	011 應臺北天籟吟社邀請，舉辦專題講座。
006 依梁秀中教授安排指導韓國女研究生。	

研究論述

001 五嶽看山座談會於中央美術學院展場。
002 文化考察團拜會中國藝術學院時合影。
003 參加中華文化總會舉辦藝文聯誼茶會。

004

005

006

007

研究論述

004　兩岸創作交流展時與王友俊教授合影。
005　前往韓國手工紙實驗所參觀研究留影。
006　海峽兩岸文化交流於顧炎武故居留影。
007　參觀山西太原雙林寺時於巨石旁留影。

001

002

003

005

006

007

008

009

展覽聯誼

001　2010臺北福華師大藝廊展覽邀請卡。
002　大風馨傳－孫家勤師生聯展現場合影。
003　中華兩岸美術學博士生創作交流展場。
004　出席袁金塔教授畫展開幕式現場合影。
005　出席陳錦芳博士畫展開幕茶會時合影。
006　臺師大57級會員聯展與吳炫三合影。
007　展覽會場與張俊傑館長及教授等合影。
008　參觀《東方綺思》於歷史博物館留影。
009　韓國李貞淑畫展與簡茂發校長等合影。

創作發表

001　靈視‧幻象—當代水墨創作展現場。
002　臺灣省城隍廟春聯書寫活動現場合影。
003　西安絲路之旅展出作品〈東風西潮〉。
004　香港首屆全球水墨畫大展時現場留影。
005　展覽會場與李奇茂教授等人現場合影。
006　展覽會場與孫家勤、羅芳等教授合影。

007　師生美展時於文學森林—紀州庵留影。
008　海峽兩岸情-臺灣書畫名家交流展場。
009　碩士畢業展時林玉山教授等蒞臨指導。
010　碩士畢業展時與鄭善禧教授現場合影。
011　與薛永年教授於中央美術學院展覽場。
012　舉辦現代荷創作展於臺北國父紀念館。

寫生旅遊

001 五嶽看山活動於北嶽恆山半山寺留影。	007 於廣西桂林龍口瀑布現場寫生時留影。
002 五嶽看山活動於西嶽華山考察時留影。	008 於蘇州虎丘風景區旅遊寫生現場留影。
003 五嶽看山活動於東嶽泰山考察時留影。	009 參觀著名鳳凰古城時於現場寫生留影。
004 五嶽看山活動於東嶽泰山南天門合影。	010 參觀著名蘇州美術館於現場寫生留影。
005 西安文化考察活動於甘肅黃河源留影。	011 貴州文化交流活動於現場寫生時留影。
006 於臺灣著名野柳風景區現場寫生留影。	012 遊歷中國西藏時於古寺壁畫現場留影。

索引圖錄——

P28
信陽光照 - 千年豔
2017　紙本設色
246×123cm

P29
早春迷濛 - 幾多紅
2017　紙本設色
246×123cm

P31
太素元清 - 極精義
2017　紙本設色
246×123cm

P31
花中有道 - 微密契
2017　紙本設色
246×123cm

P32
寒雨詩興 - 寧波行
2017　紙本設色
246×123cm

P33
感時契機 - 興中會
2017　紙本設色
246×123cm

P34
徵明幽靜 - 含真蘊
2017　紙本設色
246×123cm

P34
游心顯性 - 嚮於消
2017　紙本設色
246×123cm

P35
湛寂虛靈 - 無盡藏
2017　紙本設色
246×123cm

P36
望極河漢 - 流光吟
2017　紙本設色
246×123cm

P37
何日重遊
2016　紙本設色
177×95cm

P39
春秋烏來
2016　紙本設色
177×95cm

P40
寂寞行路
2016　紙本設色
177×95cm

P40
西府海棠
2016　紙本設色
143×76cm

P41
寧波散心
2016　紙本設色
143×76cm

P42
罔極化境
2016　紙本設色
137×69cm

P44
凝黃印記
2016　紙本設色
143×76cm

P44
無言海域
2016　紙本設色
143×76cm

P45
幾多春紅
2016　紙本設色
143×76cm

P46
石花可人
2016　紙本設色
137×69cm

P47
解夢花語
2016　紙本設色
137×69cm

P47
東方勁紅
2016　紙本設色
68×23cm

P48
零度臘梅
2016　紙本設色
68×22cm

P48
綠衣黃裡
2016　紙本設色
68×20cm

P50-51
相如賦歸
2016　紙本設色
45×69cm

P52
剎那非遠
2016　紙本設色
76×76cm

P53
使信子云
2016　紙本設色
76×76cm

P54
綺麗珊瑚
2016　紙本設色
76×76cm

P54
阿勃勒頌
2016　紙本設色
38×68.5cm

P56-57
玉樹臨風
2016　紙本設色
74×45cm×4

P58-59
中天明月
2016　紙本設色
34×68.5cm

P60-61
波瀾非信
2016　紙本設色
45×69cm

P62
（左）唯證方知
2016　紙本設色
137×35cm

P62
（中）嚮於消長
2016　紙本設色
137×35cm

P62
（右）清和當春
2016　紙本設色
137×35cm

P63
（左）無上況味
2016　紙本設色
137×35cm

P63
（中）陌上雲霓
2016　紙本設色
137×35cm

P63
（右）遊遨及此
2016　紙本設色
137×35cm

P71
揚清
2016　紙本設色
45×35cm

P84
自在當初
2016　紙本設色
69×45cm

P86
花雨
2016　紙本設色
69×45cm

P90
觀空
2016　紙本設色
69×45cm

P94
靜影沉璧
2016　紙本設色
69×45cm

P95
擬真
2016　紙本設色
69×45cm

P98
誰能會心
2016　紙本設色
34.5×23cm

P101
日上
2016　紙本設色
69×45cm

P128
顯見
2016　紙本設色
69×45cm

P129
八煙
2016　紙本設色
34×45.5cm

P132
春朝
2016　紙本設色
34×45.5cm

P137
顧盼
2016　紙本設色
69×54cm

P138-139
花東縱谷
2016　紙本設色
9×69cm

P138-139
青靄白波
2016　紙本設色
11×69cm

P99
歡・101
2014　紙本設色
143×76cm

P105
魚說那島1—
驗諸史實即可明
2014　紙本設色
136×69cm

P105
魚說那島2—
證其源由方能顯
2014　紙本設色
136×69cm

P106
魚說那島3—
有以待之昭真智
2014　紙本設色
136×69cm

P106
魚說那島4—
無住生意示正德
2014　紙本設色
136×69cm

P107
魚說那島5—
水面風波我不知
2014　紙本設色
136×69cm

P107
魚說那島6—
自由心解宜少語
2014　紙本設色
136×69cm

P108
魚說那島7—
自在性現應莫言
2014　紙本設色
136×69cm

P92
夢迴東方
2013　紙本設色
137×68cm

P64
天邊玫瑰
2012　紙本設色
246×120cm

P72
上海梧桐
2012　紙本設色
143×76cm

P79
寂寞梧桐
2012　紙本設色
143×76cm

P80
含容空有
2012　紙本設色
143×76cm

P81
新月梧桐
2012　紙本設色
143×76cm

P82
文心雕龍
2012　紙本設色
143×76cm

P85
仁愛之樹
2012　紙本設色
143×76cm

P87
問君何適
2012　紙本設色
73×76cm

P88
悟明藝象
2012　紙本設色
97×60cm

P91
風動心門
2012　紙本設色
97×60cm

P96
寂寞邊坡
2012　紙本設色
143×76cm

P124
顯見超情
2012　紙本設色
70×68cm

P126
靈的動機
2012　紙本設色
69×68cm

P127
嗨！閻浮提
2012　紙本設色
69×68cm

P83
曇花一現
2011　紙本設色
143×76cm

P65
青鳥始信
2008　紙本設色
240×120cm

P69
若有所思
2008　紙本設色
143×76cm

P69
極春倚望
2008　紙本設色
143×76cm

P70
無意春聲
2008　紙本設色
143×76cm

P70
朝元
2008　紙本設色
68×47cm

P93
荷月
2008　紙本設色
45×67cm

P97
月光寒吟
2008　紙本設色
76×70cm

P100
遠芳春意
2008　紙本設色
143×76cm

P121
藍調夜曲
2008　紙本設色
142×90cm

P122
幸運石云
2008　紙本設色
68×68cm

P124
蓮心自在
2008　紙本設色
68×68cm

P140
妙華
2008　紙本設色
68×47cm

P140
興會
2008　紙本設色
68×47cm

P141
洛神
2008　紙本設色
68×47cm

P141
迷欲
2008　紙本設色
68×47cm

P120
Mother・臺灣
2007　紙本設色
76×70cm

P123
山東日照
2004　紙本設色
60×97cm

P135
山海經驗
2004　紙本設色
46×69cm

P135
西山龍門
2004　紙本設色
46×69cm

P136
古道幻象
2004　紙本設色
46.5×68.5cm

P136
喜出望外
2004　紙本設色
46.5×68cm

P76-78
流動智慧
2002　紙本設色
142×360cm

P102
解夢花語
2002　紙本設色
59×96cm

P102
生之禮讚
2002　紙本設色
59×96cm

P103
向日朝陽
2002　紙本設色
59.5×96.5cm

P110
陽光聚會
2002　紙本設色
60×96cm

P110
恆山造象
2002　紙本設色
59×96cm

P111
光明在望
2002　紙本設色
96×59cm

P112-113
自性思維
2002　紙本設色
59×96cm

P131
黃金海岸
2002　紙本設色
45×68cm

P133
陽朔金波
2002　紙本設色
45×34cm

編者按：

　　李憶含以其獨特而鮮明自我風格形塑，映對顯性且微密的「尊重己靈」之意涵，鼇定「體時用中」的「中」，即為中庸、中觀、中和與中華之道；所謂「體時用中」，也就是體察廿一世紀的當代，要靈活運用中庸之道。「中者，天下之正道。庸者，天下之定理。」（註）

　　他的水墨創作理念與精神，重點就在於體時用中的「藝道美學」，以及任運西東之「靈動思惟」，所呈現出的風格和圖式，既是兼具東方「逸興」的情思美感，也似含容當代「神會」之理則意趣。其「凝視」、洞見生命正道及宇宙定理，儼如體證「因實在而存在」的觀照思維。

註：子程子曰：「不偏之謂中，不易之謂庸。中者，天下之正道，庸者，天下之定理。」引自中國哲學書電子化計劃網站（https://ctext.org/zh）：南宋朱熹《四書章句集注：中庸章句》

藝道美學・靈動思惟 —— 2018李憶含觀象擬眞

The Inspirational Thinking of the Aesthetics of Artistic Principle
- 2018 Lee Yi-han Simulated Images

作　　者｜　李憶含

發 行 人｜　李憶含

編　　製｜　雄獅圖書股份有限公司

總 編 輯｜　李柏黎

執行主編｜　黃長春

協力編校｜　黃怜穎、施梅珠

設　　計｜　陳紀陵

出版發行｜　李憶含藝術工作室

地　　址｜　106臺北市忠孝東路四段216巷11弄16號7F

電　　話｜　(02) 2752-9495　2741-0349

專　　線｜　0936-701702

傳　　真｜　(02) 2778-6877

網　　址｜　http://www.yihan.com.tw
　　　　　　http://weibo.com/u/3660755392

信　　箱｜　yihanart@yahoo.com.tw
　　　　　　Yihanart101@gmail.com

郵　　撥｜　帳號15409553　戶名 李憶含

攝　　影｜　林茂榮　何樹金　洪朱在

經　　紀｜　楊君玲 0938364705
　　　　　　王美智 0921841356
　　　　　　東方藝術美學研究會

印　　刷｜　永光彩色印刷股份有限公司

定　　價｜　新臺幣1600元

初　　版｜　2018年11月

I S B N｜　978-986-97008-0-1（精裝）

國家圖書館出版品預行編目（CIP）資料

藝道美學.靈動思惟：李憶含觀象擬真.2018 / 李憶含作.
-- 初版. -- 臺北市：李憶含藝術工作室, 2018.11
　面；　公分
ISBN 978-986-97008-0-1（精裝）

1. 水墨畫 2. 畫冊

945.5　　　　　　　　　　　　　　　107016895